SUNFLOWERS
FOR SUZY

Ros Rendle

SAPERE
BOOKS

SUNFLOWERS
FOR SUZY

Published by Sapere Books.

20 Windermere Drive, Leeds, England, LS17 7UZ,
United Kingdom

saperebooks.com

ISBN: 978-1-80055-619-5

CHAPTER 1

Suzy stopped, wondering which of the two roads she should take. She liked to drive, but the journey had been long enough. Eager to get to her destination, she had no wish to spend ages wandering around on the last leg. She's taken enough time in her life doing that, recently.

In the field next to the road a farmer stood on the wheel-arch of his tractor. He peered into the mechanism of the crop sprayer.

Suzy tucked her long, dark hair behind her ears, climbed out of her car and marched through the long grass in the gateway.

"*Excusez-moi?*" she called. Then she continued in her best college French, "*Bonjour*, I hope you can tell me which way to the *chambre d'hôte* of Madame Altier."

The farmer jumped off the green tractor and strode to meet her.

"I'm sorry to interrupt," Suzy added, as she smoothed her hot hands down her skirt.

The man gave a mischievous smile. Suzy thought she saw a touch of arrogance too, as he put his head on one side and his eyes travelled to her hands sliding down the seams of her skirt. His realisation that she was English made him speak slowly. He pointed and gave her basic directions in a deep, husky voice. Was he watching her too closely as he did so? He seemed kind enough in the way he responded, but was that a smile or a smirk? Suzy appraised him; his clothes were scruffy, but then he was working. His dark hair fell forwards and his teeth were a little crooked. He smiled slightly as he spoke, subtly appraising her, she thought.

"*Merci beaucoup*," Suzy replied when he'd finished speaking. She wanted to scuttle back to her car but managed to walk with nonchalance. She was sure the farmer's eyes followed her retreat.

Suzy began to drive off, and her shoulders dropped as the tension began to disappear. This expedition she had engineered was starting to work its magic at last. She didn't know its direction, but she was determined that it would lead to something better.

She took the road that the farmer had indicated. She drove past woodland and caught a glimpse of wild daffodils poking through the forest floor. The sound of a woodpecker echoed from the trees. The road undulated with the hills, but the gentle bends meant she steered with care.

Suzy drove down the narrow road with a high, steep bank on one side and fields descending away on the other. It wasn't long before she passed a sign bearing the village's name: Fleurus-le-Comte, her destination.

She crossed a small bridge and spotted a bar. She thought to go in and ask for further directions, when she saw an old man about to enter. He turned to stare as he heard the car. Suzy pulled up and through the open window she called, "*Excusez-moi?*"

The man halted. He had an extraordinary rolling gait; one leg was shorter than the other. A lined, weathered face and grizzled hair showed his age. He wore an apron over his jeans and a shabby open-necked shirt. A grimy pair of wellington boots on his feet completed the image. He put his bucket of vegetables on the ground and hobbled across to Suzy, ducking to hear her ask for directions.

Again, she received instructions and found that she was much closer than she thought. As she drove round the bend, she recognised the house from the photograph on the internet. She pulled into the wide driveway between the impressive gate pillars, then got out of the car and stretched.

The sky was blue, with a few white clouds hanging motionless. Daffodils and aubrietia drifted around and over the low walls which mounted the steps up to the front door of the house. High in the fir tree next to the car, a blackbird joyously welcomed the late afternoon.

Suzy took a deep breath, left her bags for the moment and climbed the steps. The old-fashioned bell next to the door resounded when she pulled the string.

She turned on the top step and surveyed the village. It was a good vantage point. She gazed along the road. A green tractor turned into the gates of a long, low house. It looked familiar. The attractive farmer she'd met earlier — who was too conceited for her taste — jumped down and went into the barn next to the house. Just then, the front door to the bed and breakfast opened and Suzy turned back to greet her hostess.

An elderly lady extended her hand and Suzy took it. Feeling the gnarled knuckles, she relaxed her grip.

"Madame Altier? *Je m'appelle* Suzanna Summers. Suzy."

"*Bienvenue*," said the lady warmly. "Please come in," she continued in French. "Have you no bags?"

"They're in the car. I'll fetch them. I wanted to make sure you were at home and that I had the right place," Suzy managed to say.

Madame Altier spoke basic English, but the onus would be on Suzy to speak the native language here. She enjoyed the challenge. She'd taken A-level French at school and although it was several years since then, she'd also studied the language for a time at the local college. It had stood her in good stead on the many holidays in France she had taken with her mum and dad. Even after her dad had died, for several years she and her mum had crossed the Channel for holidays together — until recently, of course.

Suzy descended to her car, heaved out her bags and locked the door. Re-mounting the steps, she entered the large living room. The table was large and heavy but the mismatched chairs all had cotton seat covers of different colours which added a gaiety to the room.

"Come this way." Madame Altier beckoned her to follow.

The room that Suzy was given smelled fragrant. The bed was enormous and made of rich, dark oak, with plump pillows and a thick duvet. A large wooden wardrobe matched the bed and an old cheval mirror stood in the corner. Madame Altier led Suzy across the room and showed her a large, light bathroom with a good-sized shower, a toilet and a handbasin. The walls were papered with a delicate green and blue pattern, and there were rugs beside the shower and the bed.

"I shall be very comfortable. Thank you," Suzy smiled.

"When you are ready, come to the living room and take a glass of wine," said Madame Altier.

Suzy put away most of her things and washed her hands. Should she phone Edward and let him know she had arrived? *No*, she thought. *All in good time.* She returned to the living room.

"Please sit." Madame Altier indicated a chair at the table.

Suzy observed the old lady. The routine now taking place was one that must have been performed countless times. Madame busied herself fetching glasses, an opened bottle from the sideboard and a small plate of crisps. As Suzy sat, she saw the stooped figure, grey curled hair and the overall and slippers worn by many other women of Madame's age and culture. She had seen countless flowery, belted housecoats like that on market stalls across the country during previous excursions.

Suzy sat still and her eyes darted, but soon she was more at ease. Before long the two of them were getting on well. They chatted and laughed over misunderstandings.

"I thought *neuf* was the word for the number nine," Suzy laughed. "I didn't realise it also meant new. I wondered why you would have nine dishwashers. I've been learning French for a while, but I still make silly mistakes."

After a glass of wine and then a top-up, Suzy became so relaxed she found herself explaining to Madame Altier one of the main reasons for her visit.

"My Mum died four months ago," Suzy confessed. "We lived together, she and I, in our family bungalow. When she became very ill, I looked after her — giving bed-baths, measuring medicines, and changing her clothes. I was always anxious about whether she was in pain, and now she's at peace I miss her. It's been hard."

"Oh, you poor dear," Madame Altier sympathised. "I remember when *ma mère* was ill as if it was yesterday." She made to pour Suzy another glass of wine. Suzy managed to put her hand on top of her glass. She had not eaten, and already she was aware of talking too much. She didn't want to disgrace herself, but this unwinding had to be good.

"I was sitting for hours on end. I watched and waited," Suzy said. She remembered her mum's eyelids fluttering. "When the final moment came, with her last breath, her body seemed to sink. I remember straightening my back and drawing a deep breath. Then I got up and stared out of the window. I didn't know what to do next. I was so lost."

Madame Altier sat still like a little wizened bird with eyes bright and sharp. Her head was on one side as she concentrated on Suzy's accented French.

"Now, in hindsight, I can see how the grief took its toll. I began to neglect my appearance. My clothes started to look loose and my hair was over-long and untidy. People at work dropped hints, but I didn't recognise their remarks as such. Then my friend Jo spoke to me. She was so good. We've known each other for years, since school. She took me in hand." Suzy smiled at the remembered conversation. "'You're only thirty-eight,' Jo told me. 'There is the odd strand of grey in your hair and its lank.' She took me to the hairdresser and then we went shopping for new clothes. I started to wear colour again."

"Well, your hair is beautiful now, *chérie*," Madame Altier said, "and high cheekbones are attractive, too. You are lucky with your looks."

Suzy frowned and shrugged. "If Mum were here now, she would peer at my face and see the lines and shadows under my eyes. She was always so careful with her complexion."

"It was my sister who took me in hand," Madame Altier said. "I've never married, and my mother used to live here with me after my sister moved away. When she died, it felt so empty. My sister wanted me to go and live with her. She's always lived on her own as well. She said I wasn't eating properly. It seems so recent, but that was years ago now. So I do know how it's been for you."

"I'm sorry, I sound so self-centred, telling you my troubles." Suzy, embarrassed at having rambled on, decided it must be the wine. She straightened her back and smiled. "Now, I'm thinking of making a major change. I might even end up living over here. That's the other reason I've come: I'm going to use this visit to find properties in the area and decide if it would be realistic or not." Suzy stood as Madame Altier nodded and started to clear the table. "I'd like to explore the village before having my evening meal."

"Yes, there will be plenty of time. Have a good walk," Madame Altier responded.

Suzy collected her gilet, left the house and strolled down the road on a mystery journey. She passed the farm with the large green tractor, but there was no-one in sight. It always amazed her that in all her time coming to France on holidays, the villages had always seemed so deserted. She wandered at will, passing long white houses with vegetable patches at the side and brick houses with the traditional white pointing and ornate window arches. There was a small field with a few sheep and a horse.

She saw the restaurant-cum-bar that she had passed earlier and made a mental note to visit one evening. She guessed the proprietor would have an ear to the ground about the locale.

Further on still she passed the church, an enormous edifice for such a small village. The cast-iron gate was ajar, and the door was open. Although tempted to look inside, Suzy decided against doing so. It was still too sunny to spend time in a gloomy, chilly interior. She would look around the graveyard another day to see all the family names of the village.

It wasn't long before she reached the river. It gushed wide and clear. Suzy could see the pebbles on the bed and tiny fish swimming into the current. The flowerboxes on the bridge were not yet planted but ready to receive the array of geraniums and greenery she knew to be typical.

Suzy stopped here and gazed down into the water. She was thinking deeply when someone approaching stopped. She swung round as she became aware of the farmer, and he acknowledged her presence with a wide grin.

"Mademoiselle, *bonsoir*, we meet again," he said in French as he extended his hand to shake hers. He was carrying a large bucket full of cabbages and leeks. "You are one of the English who are staging a takeover of our beautiful region?" He laughed. "You are staying with Madame Altier for a couple of weeks?" He spoke in his native language, but went slowly for her.

"Yes," Suzy responded shortly. *How dare he?* she thought, her cheeks reddening. *He has no idea of my plans. Takeover indeed! How rude.* Suzy paused before she continued. "I'm exploring before dinner. It's beautiful." She indicated the river and surrounding countryside with a sweep of her arm.

"Indeed," the farmer agreed, eyeing her up and down. "Welcome to our little village. I am Jean Christophe Rochefort. My wife, Maryl, and I live over there."

A wife! Poor thing, thought Suzy. Despite herself, she felt a mix of emotions. She managed a small smile. "Have you lived here long?" she enquired to fill the awkward silence.

"All my life."

Again, Suzy glimpsed his white teeth, just a little crooked but very strong, like the rest of him.

"My father farmed here before us and I was born in the town, over that way." He pointed. "We are almost all local people. If you need any advice or information, I don't mind helping. Just ask."

"Thank you," Suzy answered.

"Well, I better get these home. Enjoy your walk and I'll see you around, I expect. I hope you enjoy your stay." With that, he hefted up his bucket. Half waving, he left her following his progress with a pensive look on her face.

Suzy turned and gazed down into the rushing water. She remained there for some time before turning to continue her walk.

Just across the bridge, more houses lined the narrow lane that ran parallel to the river. Suzy looked at the wild primroses, yellow and pink, growing in the grass verges. Willow trees stood with their branches weeping into the water. A bench stood next to one tree and Suzy decided to sit for a while and soak up the clean, fresh atmosphere.

The geese behind the house to her back gave a raucous honk, making her jump and she shivered as a small breeze stole across her shoulders. Her pleasant reverie ended. Suzy looked at her watch and shook herself as she wondered about dinner.

When Suzy had finished her meal, Madame Altier asked, "Suzy, would you like to take a coffee? You are the only guest. Would you prefer to sit alone, or might I join you?"

They had a companionable chat, and it wasn't long before Madame Altier started on her favourite topic — the other villagers.

"Oh, beware," she said. "The restaurant down the road, *oh la*! His food is not good, and I don't know how clean his kitchen is. People around here do not trust him. I am warning you about that one."

Suzy nodded but said nothing.

"His wife left, you know," her hostess continued. "She couldn't stand the chaos any longer. And..." She paused for effect. "He has that young cousin of his living there. Well, who knows what goes on?"

Suzy nodded again. She swallowed a multitude of questions that bubbled. She made a non-committal reply but thought she might still like to go there to eat and discover the truth for herself. As with all villages, there were factions and gossip. Suzy did not wish to take sides. That would be too hazardous as an outsider, but it would be useful to see how things were. "I met the farmer who lives down the road earlier," Suzy said when she got the opportunity to change the subject. However, that set Madame off on another tack. His marital situation was also a matter of interest to her hostess.

"Jean Christophe is a man whose wife is a shrew and a foolish woman. It is not wise to always be so critical, as she is."

"Do they have family?" Suzy was interested in those who might be her neighbours if she decided to live here.

"No, they never had children, but I don't think Maryl ever wanted them. Who knows? It is impossible to say what goes on in another's marriage! He has a brother and his family. They are close. They live at the other end of the village, right beside the river. Since their parents died, those two boys only have each other — and their families too, of course."

There followed a diatribe on various other villagers. The mayor was now in his fourth year out of seven in his term of office. The lady who ran the AEP — the *Association Education Populaire* — had an air of grandeur as the president of this social group, according to Madame Altier. Marc, the *bricoleur* — or village handyman — who cut the verges and cleared the weeds from the river's edge was so lazy he wanted an assistant.

"One of these days his laziness will cause us real problems. You mark my words. Monsieur Demille is always talking about it." As she gave a shiver, Suzy thought she sounded too dramatic.

Suzy realised Madame Altier was a nosey old lady, but lonely too, and she clearly welcomed the opportunity to gossip. It was interesting, but after a while Suzy had listened enough. She stifled a yawn of genuine fatigue. "Well, Madame," she interjected at the first opportunity, "it has been a long day for me. I must go to my bed."

"Oh, listen to me going on. *Je suis trop bavard*," said the old lady, patting Suzy's arm. "Of course, you are tired."

Heading down the long hallway to her room, Suzy had plenty to ponder. All the talk of the restaurant and the farmer and his wife made her head buzz.

CHAPTER 2

"Madame, this *croissant* is so good," Suzy complimented her hostess the next morning. The traditional French fare with orange juice, hot chocolate, bread and homemade jam awaited her. A bowl of fruit looked fresh and inviting. She did not go hungry.

"I'm going on an adventure of exploration this morning, Madame," Suzy announced.

"Do you want food to take for lunch?"

Her breakfast experience tempted Suzy to say yes, but in the end she declined. It would be good to find a *relais* where food would be cheap, or perhaps a small *estaminet*.

When she'd finished, Suzy gathered her sunglasses, a book and a bottle of water and descended the steps at the front of the house to her car. She wound down the windows. The day promised to be fine and warm, even though it was still early springtime. She left the village and passed the farm of the Rochefort family, where she saw Jean Christophe in the yard. He waved and grinned as she drove past. She restricted herself to a small, tight smile and a slight incline of her head in response.

As Suzy climbed the steep hill, her feeling of contentment started to soar. She stopped the car in a farm track entrance at the top of the hill, retrieved her map and perused the detail. Straight away she saw that the village lay in a valley not far from the confluence of three rivers, two major and one much smaller. Suzy looked around her, getting her bearings as best she could while the map rested on the steering wheel. From her car window, she could see crops were the main land use with many fields full of sunflower leaves of the young plants. Some empty fields had grass ready to receive cows.

Deciding on a course of action, Suzy folded the map with vigour and moved off to enjoy her day. She headed for the spot of the rivers' confluence. Her paperback, a blanket and a grassy bank were all she needed. The road, no more than a farm track, wound back and forth, returning to the valley floor through woodland just breaking into leaf.

A million small wild daffodils were coming into flower. Where the sun slanted between the tree trunks, it struck the floor like gold. Suzy slowed to appreciate the view and breathed in the fresh scent of flowers, damp moss and woodland undergrowth. Every now and then, through the trees, the valley's depth appeared. She continued her steep, meandering descent.

Two of the rivers joined in a tumble of noisy water that flowed down the valley. The map showed the third river joined just after this spot. The water here was green and white, and on its surface floated twigs and catkin flowers that it had gathered along its way. The grass, soft and springy, looked as inviting as a cushion, and there was no other soul in sight.

Suzy spread her blanket. She lay with her eyes closed. The brightness of the sun pierced her eyelids. She very nearly drifted off with the warmth, the sound of the river and the fresh smells of the open countryside all around her.

She lay and read until the book drooped and she dozed. After a while, her phone buzzed in her pocket. Retrieving it, she looked at the screen. It was Edward. She gave a guilty sigh and took the call.

"Hello, Edward," she answered.

"Suzy, thank God! You're okay, are you?"

"Yes, of course," she replied, quelling her tetchiness.

"When you didn't call, I began to wonder if you had arrived alright."

"Well, I did say I'd call you in a few days, once I got settled," she said.

"But you might have just messaged to say you were safe," Edward persisted.

"Edward, we had this discussion before I left. Okay, we've been seeing each other for a while, but you know I'm thinking of moving here for a time. You could move to the branch in Lille, but you said you weren't sure you wanted to. So I can't see where this can go." Suzy sighed. She hadn't told Madame Altier about Edward. This was why she had needed to get away, to help see things more clearly. "Sorry," she conceded, although at that moment she felt more resentful than apologetic. "I'm fine. The journey was uneventful, and I arrived in good time." She went on to give him a brief description of her accommodation and enough about her hostess to keep him happy. "I'll update you again in a few days. I'm not phoning every day. We don't speak each day as a rule. You did say you would give me space," she reminded him.

After they'd said goodbye, Suzy thought about Jo. She was the only person who would understand. Hadn't she been saying for months that Suzy should say goodbye to Edward and move on? She thought back to that last outing with him.

That evening, the doorbell had rung at precisely 7.30pm. Suzy had greeted Edward and pasted on a smile. He stood there in his corduroy jacket and smart trousers. His smooth, short hairstyle with its receding hairline and his polished shoes were just too perfect. All of a sudden, she could perceive him as others might, certainly as her friend Jo did.

It was a moment of déjà-vu. Wasn't this the same scene as the previous Saturday evening? Edward stood in this spot at the same time, holding out an identical sized bunch of flowers from the local supermarket.

"Edward. They're beautiful, as usual," Suzy said to him, accepting his offering.

"And you look smart," complimented Edward.

"Come in while I find my shoes and jacket." Before he had the opportunity to speak, Suzy volunteered, "Shall we have a glass of wine before we go?" Was this the embryo of rebellion to come?

"We don't have time for that," he responded.

"Shall we go mad and forego the film; chill out here and get a takeaway?" She suggested this on the spur of the moment.

"Well…" He hesitated. "I'm not sure about the takeaway! That's a plastic kind of alternative. If you don't fancy the film we planned, we could always go to the multiplex and watch something else."

"No. It's okay. Let's do as we said." She sighed.

"If you're sure," Edward responded. "Are you alright? You seem distracted."

"I'm fine," she reassured him, touching his arm. "I'm starting to think forwards again."

"Right." He hovered for a moment. "Shall we go?"

"Mmm." She slipped on her heeled shoes and reached for her jacket. Edward took it to help her into it, inexorably polite.

Two hours later, Edward and Suzy emerged from the cinema into the early spring air. She was in a thoughtful mood. Edward took her arm and linked it through his companionably. Or was it like her dad used to do when she was a teenager? They headed for the restaurant around the corner.

Once seated, Suzy began, "Edward I…"

"I…" he started at the same time.

"After you," she said.

"No. You go first. I have a feeling there's something you want to get out in the open."

"Yes," she murmured. Looking at his smooth face with its slightly pink cheeks, she avoided his eyes. "I… Well, I need a change. After Mum and everything."

"Oh!" He sighed and blew out his cheeks. "I'm wondering if this is going to be the big elbow speech. You know — the Dear John thing." He continued in a hurry, "A holiday would do us both good. What do you fancy? Greece? Spain? What about Florida?"

"I don't mean a holiday," she said, looking at her hands, which were twisting in her lap.

Edward looked puzzled, then bemused, then worried. "Well, what then?"

"I need a big change, a life change."

A startled look was replaced by a big smile on his face. Suzy realised, with a sudden horror, that he might have thought she was referring to progressing their relationship. She rushed on. "I need to sell the bungalow, maybe change my job. A spell abroad might be the answer."

Edward frowned. "What are you talking about?"

"I hardly know myself yet," she answered. "I need to make a change for a while, until I know what I do want."

"I don't pretend to fathom what on earth you mean," said Edward, still frowning. "Perhaps we'll discuss this when you've had time to think it through. I can't be chasing around the world right now. I have clients to consider."

"Yes, I understand," Suzy said. "I'm sorry. Those last months with Mum were so awful and so peculiar at the same time. Edward, please, I just need some space of my own for a while."

Back in the present, on the riverbank, Suzy rang Jo's number but frustratingly it went to voicemail. She spoke, hoping Jo would ring her back soon.

Back in her car, Suzy climbed a very steep, winding road. In all directions, there was no sign of human movement at all. There were no houses, no cars, no electricity pylons, nothing but vast expanses of fields and thickets of trees across the undulating landscape. Stopping the car again and switching off the engine, Suzy listened. Then, close by, a skylark pierced the silence as it soared higher and higher. Its small body disappeared into the blue, and only its voice remained on the still air.

After a satisfying lunch in a restaurant off a bar in a very tiny hamlet, Suzy followed a different route but headed back towards her own village. She smiled to herself. She had been here only twenty-four hours but already she felt at home.

Back at the B&B Madame Altier offered her coffee, but Suzy couldn't cope with another denunciation of the neighbours. She took her paperback and the remains of her bottled water and headed for the stone bench seat that she had spotted at the front of the house. The sun continued to shine. Her book remained closed on her lap as she sat idly and looked across the village. Once or twice a tractor passed, and the occupant nodded at her. An old man staggered along the road — towards the churchyard, she supposed. He had a pot plant in one shrivelled hand and a stick for support in the other. She heard chickens and a dog in the distance, but other than that all was quiet and still. Her eyes strayed to the farmhouse just down the road, but there was no sign of life there.

This brought to mind her earlier conversation with Edward. Part of her felt mean and guilty, but the rest of her was annoyed. He had broken into her isolation when he knew she needed time on her own to sort herself out. After all, before she had left, he had reluctantly agreed in the end that she should have this breathing space. Was he going to cause trouble after all?

The days progressed. Sometimes, Suzy wandered the lanes around the village or drove out to explore the region. She gathered bits of information during her stay relating to houses, banking and car registration. She was feeling increasingly in tune with the village.

There were plenty of sites relating to history and culture. She visited the large city of Arras and marvelled at its city hall and beautiful architecture. She even visited the *boves* under the city; the network of tunnels used during the First World War which were now a museum. The wax that had melted on the chalk pillar used as a makeshift altar was a poignant reminder of the war years.

On the fourth evening of Suzy's stay, there was to be a *lotto* night in the little village hall, the *Salle des Fêtes*. Suzy would not normally have enjoyed the thought of bingo, but her landlady was insistent.

"Oh, you must come," Madame Altier had said. "Everyone will be there. It will be a chance for you to meet most of them. People know you are staying here now. They will expect you. We shall go together," she added, brooking no argument.

Suzy discovered that she felt excited to be going out. She sussed out that the relaxed dress code meant wearing her jeans and a shirt was acceptable.

"There's a chill in the air tonight," Madame Altier said as she closed the door behind them. Suzy agreed and was glad she had on her wool jacket.

The *Salle* was down the road and as they entered, it enchanted Suzy. Inside the wooden building there were oak beams and a huge pot-bellied wood burner pumping out remarkable warmth and a welcoming glow. Tables and chairs filled the room, and at the furthest end locals already sat at the bar with glasses of wine and beer. Tables were being reserved here and there by those present. Madame Altier took Suzy by the arm and steered her across the room. A dark-haired lady, who seemed the same age as Suzy, occupied it.

"May we sit here?" Suzy's companion asked.

"*Certainement,*" answered the younger lady, indicating the seats as she stood to receive the customary kisses. Suzy was uncertain how to greet people, so she stuck out her hand and gave a generous smile. Before Madame Altier had time to introduce Suzy, her table companion took her hand and enquired, "You are the lady from England?" As Suzy nodded, the woman continued, "You must meet Harriet. She is English too and lives in the village. She's on her own because her partner died."

"Thank you, that would be interesting," replied Suzy. "I only have one more week until I return home. The time is passing so quickly, I'm not sure I'm ready to go yet. It is so calm and peaceful here — friendly too."

Just then, Jean Christophe appeared with glasses in his hands. "Hello, again," he greeted Suzy. "I see you have met Maryl, *ma femme.*"

"Hello," said Suzy. "Yes, we have just met, but I didn't realise this was your wife." Feeling flustered, Suzy turned back to Maryl. With a nervous laugh, she added, "Madame Rochefort, *bonsoir.*" So, this was the poor woman who had to put up with the conceit of that man.

"Jean Chri did not tell me you had met," Maryl said.

"Oh, I just asked for directions the day I arrived," Suzy answered.

"Allow me to buy you both a drink," Jean Chri said. He flashed a smile and winked at Madame Altier.

My goodness, he thinks a lot of himself, Suzy thought.

When he returned from the bar area, the room had filled. His brother, Pascal, joined the table with his wife, Amélie, and his young daughter, Melodie.

The little girl approached and kissed Suzy in welcome. "Can I go and see Anne?" she asked her mother.

"*Oui*, Melodie. But if you young ones go outside, remember that you all stay inside the fence. I shall come to check in three minutes."

"*Oui, Maman, bien sûr.*" Melodie hurried away, followed by a trio of little lads, her blonde plaits bouncing as she skipped.

The general conversation included Suzy until the games began. Numbers were called in French, of course.

"This is a real test for me to keep up," Suzy said to anyone who listened.

Pascal sat next to her, but it was Jean Christophe who kept an eye on her cards too.

"You have missed this one," he whispered and reached across to mark a number.

There was merriment at her expense. She didn't mind because it was good-natured. The break for refreshments was halfway through the evening.

Suzy asked the general company, "May I offer a donation since I haven't paid?"

"No, no," they all echoed.

"My family dealt with that after you arrived. You are a guest," Jean Christophe said.

"Well, I insist that I buy a round of drinks instead, then," she replied, which satisfied everybody.

Melodie, Pascal's daughter, reappeared with her friend Anne in time for something to eat. The men discussed together, calling across the room to someone else, something to do with planting sugar beet, Suzy thought. The women included her in their general chat. It was a relaxed and comfortable atmosphere. Maryl was quiet but polite to Suzy. Animation and encouragement glowed in Amélie's face, and she helped Suzy when she struggled with the language.

Everyone bought a ticket for the raffle and there was much laughter when Suzy won a prize and waved her ticket, shouting out, "*J'ai le billet.*" She was very puzzled by the reaction until Jean Chri explained, his eyes twinkling.

"If you are a *salope*, a tart, a slut, you say you have *le billet*. This is the bottom dollar." He added the last phrase in attractive broken English. "Here you must say *j'ai le ticket.*"

He's sniggering at me when I'm doing my best, Suzy thought privately. *He's such an ill-mannered man.* She put her hand to her mouth to stifle her embarrassment and apologised to the room, but everyone was forgiving and laughed with her rather than at her.

The evening ended with a round of handshakes and kisses.

"Thank you for a lovely evening," Suzy said to both the Rochefort families.

Before they parted, each one leaned in to kiss her too, making her a genuine part of the group. Maryl kissed beside her face on each side as protocol demanded and wished her a pleasant return journey. As Jean Chri leant towards her, she caught a mild hint of his lemon-scented aftershave and her stomach flipped. Resolutely ignoring this, she turned to Madame Altier and asked, "Are you ready to leave?"

"Yes, yes, let's go home. Perhaps we will have a little bedtime drink?" Madame Altier took Suzy's arm in a conspiratorial fashion.

The night was chill with bright stars as they made their way up the road. The lights that shone on the steeple captured the white underside of a barn owl's wings as it left the belfry.

When indoors, Madame Altier gave Suzy no time to demur from the nightcap. "Pass the bottle, my dear," she said as she reached for the glasses. "This is so nice, to have a little company. I hope you are enjoying your stay. You fit in so well here."

"It's wonderful," agreed Suzy.

"So, are you still thinking of making a more permanent move?"

"It is very tempting, but I have no means of supporting myself. The proceeds from the sale of my mother's house in England — when I sell it — will not last forever. If I had to rent here or even buy a small place, I should need work." Suzy sighed.

"Well, you never know what might turn up," the old lady said, winking.

CHAPTER 3

Madame Altier's house was long and low, known as a *longère*. It was nestled in the hillside at the centre of the village, giving the guests a view of the top of the *mairie*, which dealt with the village's administration, and the *Salle des Fêtes* with its little field for celebrations. On the other side was the church. This meant that Madame Altier always had her finger on the pulse of the village.

Breakfast was served in the enormous living room. Suzy loved the vast inglenook fireplace with the wood-burner and the logs stacked on each side. She inhaled the aroma of resin as the wood dried. Down the room, the table could seat a dozen people. There was plenty of space for all Madame's guests to take their orange juice, bread or croissants and coffee or hot chocolate.

"You have a great collection of family mementoes," Suzy said to Madame Altier.

"Some are useful and others just decorative. Many of them belonged to my grandmother or those born before her. Long, long ago we acquired them."

"The time is passing. I shall be sorry to leave." Suzy sighed. "It's as if I have found a place I really like. I want to find out more about everybody."

As Suzy gazed down at the village through the window, she followed the progress of Jean Christophe Rochefort as he came from the back of his barn. Maryl followed. From the position of her hands on her hips and the way she leaned forwards as she spoke, Suzy gathered that she was having her say. Madame Altier had intimated when Suzy had arrived that

Maryl was a scold, but then Suzy felt she had much with which to contend.

Jean Christophe stood and listened to what Suzy could not hear Maryl saying.

"It's always the same with you," she berated him. "You're always out working! Oh yes, there's time for that, but if I want something you can't do it. I wash, I clean, and I cook. All I want is to go shopping and maybe have lunch."

"This is what brings the money, though, and we had lunch out on Sunday," Jean Chri responded. "If I didn't do this, you would have no money to shop anyway." He smiled, trying hard to take any sting out of his words. "Why don't you telephone Hélène and drive across to visit her? You haven't been for a while, and you could set up a shopping session with her instead of with me."

Maryl huffed. "I might," she said. "There's nobody else in this godforsaken place I want to mix with. If I'm not here, that's where I shall be, I suppose."

Jean Christophe shrugged. He sighed as he climbed up into his tractor and backed out. *At least Pascal and his family are coming tomorrow*, he thought.

His expression softened as he thought of his little niece, four years old and as blonde as he was dark. She spoke with her hands in the most expressive way and could charm the birds out of the trees with her laughter. She lived life with a very infectious sparkle. He so looked forward to their visits.

The next day no chainsaws whirred, no lawns were being cut, no strimmers whined. The village had decreed these *outillage thermique* not to be used on Sundays. Tractors and hunting were still allowed. It being late March, though, the season was closed for everything, and so no staccato bangs broke the peace of the beautiful day.

At eleven o'clock an ancient blue Citroën car pulled up in front of the farmhouse and Jean Christophe's brother, Pascal and his wife, Amélie, climbed out. While they only lived at the other end of the village in a little house bordering the river, it was rare to witness them walking. It might be late, anyway, when they wanted to return, and they didn't want to carry their daughter home.

Amélie opened the rear door of the car. Out hopped the beautiful blonde child with an ancient stuffed toy dog in her arms. Jean Chri opened the front door with an expansive grin on his face. The child ran as fast as her little legs would carry her, flinging herself with absolute trust into her uncle's arms. He swung her and her little dog up and around in a whirl of mutual joy.

"Melodie, *ma mignon*," Jean Chri greeted her. He smiled at the others. "It's so good to see you again."

"Hello, little brother," responded Pascal. "Though not so little," he added, looking up at Jean Chri and eyeing his shoulders and large, capable hands.

This farm was Pascal's birthright, but he didn't envy the farmer's life and Jean Chri loved it. He did, however, enjoy the great outdoors as the owner of a small bark recycling and treatment business. He much preferred the regular hours. For the two brothers and their families to share a Sunday meal was normal. It was a family day and since their parents had died, they often got together and ate as they had always done throughout their youth.

Pascal understood his brother's circumstances. They'd shared confidences from an early age. "How's it going?" he asked with sympathy as Amélie took Melodie's hand and headed for the front door, where Maryl stood waiting. The brothers watched them go; two blonde heads, one bending to the other to share a laughing comment.

"Much the same," answered Jean Chri. "The calves need to be outside soon," he added, delaying the response that Pascal wanted.

"Oh, come on, little brother," Pascal sighed. "I wish you had a family too. It's a joy and gives such a sense of wellbeing."

"If Maryl had agreed to a child, perhaps then she would have something more meaningful to occupy her time. She doesn't seem happy with anything else here. She might be less irritable. Yes, I do want children but Maryl does not."

"Did you ask her if it frightened her, as we discussed last time? She's younger than you. It's not too late."

"She denied it when last we spoke of it. She must think it will be more work than she can undertake. I stressed I would share everything, as far as I can. I appreciate she has to do the hardest work involved, carrying and giving birth. No matter how patient I try to be, in the end I am forced to make sharp remarks. It makes no difference." Jean Chri frowned.

Was it his fault? He didn't know. He tried to reassure her of his love, and he tried hard to please her. He stared for a moment into the distance as he remembered a time before they'd married, nearly ten years ago. She'd always seemed reserved, finding it difficult to express her feelings, but he thought he understood her. The daughter of a farmer, she was familiar with the life. Indeed, working from home, he was around quite a bit. He tried to divide his time between the needs of his wife and those of the farm.

"However much I do, it is never enough."

Maryl had been slim and lovely, and Jean Chri still thought that when he surveyed her face and body. He didn't notice the line deepening between her eyes or the droop of her mouth becoming more frequent.

"I've never looked for satisfaction or companionship outside my marriage, you know that. We go out and I buy her little gifts. I give her attention and reassurance. I can't take it. I'm aware that I am arguing back much more. She's not happy either, though."

"Mind you," Pascal added, with a smile, "at five o'clock in the morning when Melodie wakes up full of energy, I'm not so sure about children bringing a feeling of wellbeing." He chuckled, relieving the sombreness of the moment.

"Well, there we have it," said Jean Chri. Then, changing the subject, he said, "Let's go in and find an *apéro*. We've set the table outside today, since it's so warm." They walked through the house. He opened the waiting bottle for the adults and poured an orange juice for Melodie.

"Help yourselves." He indicated to the little snacks waiting as the *aperitif*.

"Can I go and say hello to the calves?" asked Melodie.

"Of course, *ma petite bijou*," responded her uncle.

"She's been asking about them all the way here," said Pascal. "She wants one for a pet at home, and I had to remind her that they grow awfully large. She's desperate for a pet."

The two wives disappeared to sort out the dinner and Jean Chri and Pascal wandered after Melodie. They found her, not in the cow barn, but on the edge of the grass near the hedge.

"Look," she shouted. "Look what I've found!"

The men went to admire whatever it was she had found. Melodie had discovered a dead mole on the surface of the soil. It didn't appear mauled or unpleasant and she was both intrigued and delighted. The grey-brown fur on its body was soft as she stroked it gently with one finger. It had tiny blind eyes and its ears were covered in fur too. The claws were long and dense-looking, and its little snout was pointed and pink.

"Poor little thing," she sighed. "Can I have it for a pet?"

"That wouldn't be a good idea." Her papa smiled. His child was learning about life … and death. "After a while he would not be so attractive."

"Why?" Melodie enquired.

Jean Chri decided to avoid going down that route. "Let's make a comfy place in the soft, warm earth for him, shall we? I know a calm and peaceful place."

The family ate well into the afternoon. The lamb was cooked to perfection, being pink in the centre and very tender. Jean Chri helped carry the dishes outside and then carved the meat. The vegetables had tasty dressings, and the roast potatoes were crispy on the outside and soft and fluffy within. It was three o'clock before the delicious cheeses came. There had been Maroilles, which smelt awful but tasted soft and tangy, a local Sire de Créquy and a Camembert. After the dessert, there was coffee: the small flavourful espresso so loved by the French.

"Melodie has such a sunny personality," Jean Chri said.

"She's used to playing on her own. She is happy to occupy herself in the garden, gathering daisies," Amélie responded. "We often make them into a chain."

The afternoon passed pleasantly in the warmth of the spring sunshine. The mole was laid beneath the grass in a quiet corner. Melodie scattered flower petals and was satisfied. All four adults chatted, and peace reigned between Maryl and Jean Christophe.

As the sun slid down the sky and behind the top of the steep hills, Pascal and Amélie collected up a drowsy Melodie.

"Time to go." Pascal looked at his watch.

"She has got Choupinette, hasn't she?" Amélie reassured herself. "She cannot go to bed without him, scruffy as he is."

Her toy dog was found, and she clutched it in her arms and stroked its fur with her thumb. She snuggled into her father's arms as he lifted her to kiss her aunt and uncle goodbye.

After the guests had left, Jean Chri helped Maryl clear away the last of the dishes and cups. He felt more relaxed than he had for quite some time.

"That was a delicious dinner, as always. I am lucky, indeed, to have such an accomplished wife," he said.

"Hmmph," was her only response.

They were just finishing their tasks when Madame Altier arrived, knocking at the front door. Maryl answered. "*Madame, bienvenue*," she said, leaning to exchange the customary kisses.

"Maryl," Madame Altier said, "I'm so sorry to trouble you, on a Sunday too. I have a problem with the handle of my bedroom door, and I've tried to fix it, but I am quite unable. I wondered if Jean Christophe might help me?"

"Jean Chri," called Maryl, indicating that Madame Altier should step into the house.

"*Bonsoir*," acknowledged Jean Chri before moving to kiss the visitor's cheeks.

Madame Altier explained her problem. "I'm worried that I shall get stuck in my room." She showed her gnarled hands.

"Of course, I'll come and look. Just let me get my tools."

They walked to the Bed and Breakfast together and Jean Chri began his work on the door handle. It was a simple matter and he soon fixed it.

"Will you take a glass?" Madame Altier enquired afterwards.

Jean Chri hesitated but then decided that he would. "Is your English lady still staying?"

"She's going the day after tomorrow. She's gone out for a walk."

Jean Chri was surprised when he felt a little deflated.

"But I think she may return. I understand she might well consider moving to this area."

"There may be one or two who have something to say about another English person settling here, Monsieur Demille for one. So, you have further guests coming quite soon?" Jean Chri asked to deflect any further conversations about neighbours.

They chatted for a while, and then Madame Altier dropped her surprise announcement. "The way I'm going, I might not be able to stay much longer. My hands are so painful, and my sister keeps saying I should go to her. I'm not sure I want to, though. I was born here. It would be a wrench."

"I know, Madame," Jean Chri responded, "but there is always someone here to help you out."

"You are kind." She leaned over and patted his hand. "We shall see, we shall see. I don't like to ask for help all the time and it's quite tiring, this little business."

"There are always decisions to make in this life. You with your sister, the English lady, and me … well…" He shrugged and stood to leave.

CHAPTER 4

As Suzy passed the restaurant door on one of her strolls, it opened and the older man with the rolling gait she had seen on her arrival appeared.

"Mademoiselle Summers," he said, extending his hand to shake.

Clearly people have been talking. He knows my name and yet he was not at the lotto evening, Suzy thought. "Please, call me Suzy. My name is Suzanna, but I don't like it so Suzy is better."

"And I am Jerome," said the man. "You may have heard of me from Madame Altier," he added, pulling a face.

Suzy nodded and smiled.

"How have you settled in?"

"It's fine so far. I am enjoying my visit." Suzy saw no sense in taking sides in a petty village argument. She was determined to be even-handed with everyone.

As they were chatting, another lady came along the street and waved a greeting to Jerome. It transpired that she, too, was English. With a tall and sturdy figure, she was striking. Her complexion was smooth and clear and she had short hair, light in colour. Her nose was fine and straight, and her generous mouth gave her a sensual look. This emphasised her presence as she strode across the road with the gait of an athlete. As she walked, however, her wide blue eyes darted as if she was unsure of herself.

Jerome took charge of the situation and introduced the newcomer as Harriet. "Harriet lives on *rue de la Vieille Curé* along by the river."

"Yes, it's right on the riverbank; the little white house with the clay stork on the large stump by the door," she added. "You must be Suzanna Summers. I've heard about you. Pleased to meet you." She smiled and extended her hand in a no-nonsense manner.

"Please, call me Suzy."

"Why don't you both come in and have a glass of wine," Jerome said. *"C'est la maison qui régale."*

On the house, Suzy thought. *How welcoming.*

Suzy and Harriet looked at each other and smiled in agreement, and in that instant Suzy knew that she had an ally. "Thank you," she said.

As they entered the restaurant, Suzy looked around at the strange antiquated darkness of the place. There was no-one else there at this early afternoon hour. Jerome went behind the massive oak bar and pressed the old-fashioned cassette recorder button to play quiet music.

He poured three glasses of wine while Suzy and Harriet took a seat at a small table in the bay window. Harriet arranged her long flowered skirt, seemingly nervous of her present company, though she remained friendly. Jerome took a cloth from the bar top and went behind to dry some glasses, joining the conversation from his position.

"Have you lived here for long?" Suzy asked.

"It will soon be eleven years," Harriet answered. "Before someone else tells you, my partner died three years ago. We'd been together ever since leaving school, but she got cancer."

Suzy was sorry to hear the story, and Harriet had her sympathy and admiration straight away.

"Moving on…" Harriet said, shrugging and turning to the bar.

Jerome spoke to another much younger man who'd entered the room via a door behind the bar. "This is Éric, my cousin." He made the introductions.

Éric nodded at Suzy and Harriet, and following a nudge from Jerome he came and kissed Harriet on each cheek and extended his hand to Suzy. Then he moved to the end of the long table which ran down the centre of the whole room, and began folding a pile of paper serviettes.

"*Que tu fais?*" Jerome asked him. "They don't go like that, I told you so many times." He laughed. "We fold them like this now; we must be refined to keep up."

Harriet leaned forwards and whispered to Suzy in English: "Jerome likes to think of himself as sophisticated. He worked in the kitchens of an hotel in the small market town fifteen kilometres from the village. He thinks it a much bigger place than this small spot. It was many years before he opened this restaurant bar of his own."

Suzy's gaze flicked to Éric, who was almost as round as he was tall.

"I don't know if that is his natural figure," Harriet said, following Suzy's eyes. "There is speculation among the locals that it's all the undergarments and jumpers he wears. Even in high summer he wears a towel around his neck and can often be seen with a woolly hat on. It is to protect him from the sun, so he maintains."

Suzy smiled.

"There is talk of issues surrounding the relationship of these cousins and their restaurant. But they have both been so kind and helpful to me. It bothers me not one jot what they do. I'd be the last one to judge," Harriet said with feeling.

"You have to take as you find," Suzy said.

"Exactly."

"Éric, fetch the cutlery, please, and we'll set the table for the Jourdon party," Jerome said.

Éric trundled off to the kitchen and Jerome surveyed his domain. The chill in the air ensured the fire was lit already. The corn cobs for the chickens were drying, hanging by their stalks to one side of the enormous fireplace.

As Éric returned with the knives and forks, Jerome said, "I'm just going outside to fetch another *faggot* for the fire." On his return, he frowned to see Éric standing beside the table with the knives and forks still in his hands. With patience, he remarked, "Lay the table now, Éric, for the Jourdon party."

Seeing Suzy's curious expression, Harriet leaned forward again. "It was unfortunate. Éric did his National Service for France in the year 2000. It involved ten months, which he just completed before compulsory military service ended a year later. That's one year earlier than first planned by the government, so he was unlucky in that respect. After his return, he was ill. It was a mystery to the rest of the village. They wondered if something had happened or whether he had experienced or seen something terrible during his time in the army. There were all kind of rumours."

"I'm beginning to understand this place is rife with rumours and gossip."

"That is true. I sound as if I've fallen into the same trap."

"It's helpful for me to know about these people, though," Suzy said.

"Well, Éric went away again for several months. When he returned, he was still in a right state, unable to think or do anything for himself. He kept falling asleep with his head on the table. It was odd and caused gossip when Jerome gave him a home, since Éric has closer family in the same village. His own father lives just at the other end of the main street. The difference in the ages of the cousins means that Jerome is more like a dad to Éric. They each came from enormous families. Jerome is the eldest of twelve siblings and Éric is the second youngest in his family, hence the age difference between the two."

"Put a knife and fork out for each place and then fetch the glasses from under the bar," Jerome reminded Éric now.

The younger man shambled around the table as instructed, while Jerome watched him with a patient, kindly eye.

"I'm going to lay out the *apéro*, Éric," he said. "You finish the table, *oui?*"

There was no response.

"Éric, finish the table?" Jerome prompted.

"*Oui, oui,*" Éric said as Jerome headed out to the kitchen.

"Harriet and Suzy, come and look at this." Jerome beckoned them to follow him.

The kitchen was dark and cluttered. There were pans in the sink ready for washing, and the huge oven took up half of one wall.

Jerome had a peek in the fridge. "Here, look. What do you think?"

There was an enormous whole salmon that he had cooked and dressed.

"It looks magnificent," Harriet said, and Suzy agreed.

"I need to arrange the finger food *aperitifs* on those large serving plates, ready for the family to nibble on while they all arrive," Jerome explained.

They left the kitchen to finish their drinks and Harriet explained Jerome's particularity. "This is a family who frequent Jerome's restaurant often, so he knows they will not be as critical as some of the others who live around here. One or two have turned the knife and are the main reason for Jerome's current financial problems. He's told me this. Rumours have been tricky to cope with, although Jerome is unsure of the main reason. He had to deal with Monsieur Pierron and his plump, greasy wife. They accused him of substituting the lobster they ordered and paid for with shredded crab-stick, for their son's confirmation celebration. That was mild, though, considering what some people are suggesting."

"He has a lot to put up with," Suzy advanced.

"Yes, he does, and yet he's so kind and thoughtful to many of us. As you said, you have to take as you find."

Jerome came through, carrying the *apéro* dishes. Then he wiped his hands on his apron and smiled to himself, pleased with what he had created.

Suzy and Harriet thanked him and took their leave. At the door, Suzy halted.

"What's this?" She indicated a piece of card tacked to the back of the door.

"The *ducasse*," Harriet said, reading the handmade poster. "Most of the villages have one. It's the celebration gathering that happens in May; the largest event of the year. Everyone sits for an extravaganza of feasting and fun with games and quite a bit of drinking." She laughed. "Alain Ducasse was the first chef to own restaurants carrying three Michelin stars in three different cities. He acquired the most stars during his career. The village *ducasse* is an acknowledgement of this level of expertise, though the event itself is just an excuse for rollicking good fun, if you ask me. For Jerome, it must be his major source of income. He's provided the catering for several years now. If he lost that contract, it might force the closure of his business. Or so he has hinted."

"Well, thanks. It's been great meeting you." Suzy meant every word.

"You too," Harriet agreed. "I don't think I've talked so much in one go for ages."

On the spur of the moment Suzy had a thought. "Hey, I don't suppose you fancy coming here to eat tomorrow night do you? I did say to Jerome I would before I leave, but I'd rather have company."

"That would be lovely. Shall I pop back in and tell him?"

"Yes. Thank you."

"Until tomorrow, then. About eight?"

The next evening, Harriet and Suzy were seated at the long table. Another couple, who Harriet had greeted as they arrived, sat at the other end. As Suzy sat, she looked under the table and then gave Harriet a quizzical look. Running for most of its length was a tree trunk which seemed to extend into the open fire and was the basis of the flames, which danced. "I know," Harriet said as she followed Suzy's gaze. "It's unique but practical, I suppose."

At that moment, Jerome, still wearing the same apron he'd had on in the kitchen, arrived with an axe and Suzy was amazed when he swung the blunt side of the blade against the far end of the log, causing sparks to erupt and the flames to leap higher as it shifted into them. The couple at that end of the table simply turned their heads and nodded smilingly towards him.

The door opened and two young men came in. They approached Harriet and kissed her on each cheek as she stood to receive their greeting. She introduced them to Suzy and they came around the table and kissed her, too, before heading over to the bar to order a drink.

Harriet explained in English to Suzy. "They are brothers, Alexandre is twenty and Nicolas is nineteen. They still live at home with their mum and dad and their two much younger sisters, Elodie and Collette.

"*Salut*," Nicolas said as they shook hands with Jerome at the bar.

"There's a beer for each of you," Jerome said. "On the house."

"Thanks," said Alexandre. "Our house is always so crowded."

"And not comfortable," added Nicolas.

Harriet whispered to Suzy, "In true French country style, everything happens in the single living room at their house. The dining table and the wooden chairs take up most of the space. There's just room for one comfortable armchair but it's very battered.

"Their father commandeers the chair since he gets in from work first. That's fair enough, but if Elodie is arguing with their mum again, it's not possible to watch anything on the television, they say. Nicolas told me that at least here they have space to talk boys' talk and drink a beer in comparative peace and quiet."

Suzy nodded her understanding.

"They've formed a habit of dropping in here after work and before their family supper. Both boys work as farmhands for different large enterprises in the local area. These farms are mixed agriculture, with both crops and cattle."

"I've seen that, as I've driven or walked around. I bet the sunflowers are stunning in July." Suzy took a forkful of the delicious stew that had arrived at their table.

"They are indeed. The farm owner deals with the cows but needs help all year round with the crops. The boys drive tractors and harvesters and they've each become skilled in manoeuvring large pieces of farm equipment. There are trailers, ploughing mechanisms and spreaders, seed drills and balers. In their own way they're skilled, but the work involves long hours and poor pay. It takes the joint income of the adults in the family to keep them solvent. It's a confined lifestyle with neither boy getting out much, never mind meeting girls and having much of a social life outside the village."

"I bet Jerome's always pleased to see them. I see he gave them a free beer. It can't be good for his profits, but I guess he welcomes the company."

"Yes indeed. He likes looking after Éric; it satisfies his need to care, since his wife took the family away, but it must be wearisome."

"So, what's up with Monsieur Demille?" Alexandre was asking now.

Suzy couldn't help listening as Harriet ate her meal.

"I've no idea," responded Jerome. "What do you mean?"

"He and Madame Altier were having a right good gossip this lunchtime when I went out to unload the wood from the trailer. I could hear them through the hedge out on the road. She said the word disgrace and the name of this place." He laughed and shook his head, taking the sting out of his words. "Then he was ranting about the English and how they are all moving here and buying up property. They must have realised I was there after that; it all went quieter. I know they were still blethering, though."

"Monsieur Demille would rather I closed. I have no idea why — I've never done anything to him," Jerome said. "But Madame Altier, she just doesn't want the competition. She's expensive, though, for what she offers. That's what I understand. Her vegetables are not too fresh either. The desserts are just pots from the *supermarché*."

"There's no love lost between them. Madame Altier was good friends with Jerome's ex-wife, Hélène." Harriet, who had obviously overheard the conversation too, explained to Suzy in a soft voice.

"Hélène departed after one final heated row about the state of the kitchen. She liked to dominate that area. As with many wives of her generation, she believed she should run the household, including the domestic arrangements for the restaurant-bar. Jerome was clear that this was his work and she had no place interfering with his arrangements, no matter how chaotic his management was. It was all round the village. He produces good food using fresh vegetables, meat and fish. Most of the meat's so fresh it's been running around the yard not one hour earlier than the preparation requires." She chuckled. "His organisation leaves much to be desired, though, and his wife couldn't stand for it. She moved out and took the three children with her. They went to live with her parents several years ago, and she's never set foot in the village again."

"I bet the villagers had much to say on the subject," Suzy ventured. "Everyone has an opinion and a side to take in matters like this."

"Yes, and these divides persist over time until few remember the initial cause of the rift, particularly in a small village like this."

The door opened again, and an upright figure walked to the bar.

"That's Monsieur Demille," Harriet said.

Like many of the inhabitants of such villages, he was of the older generation. He still wore blue working dungarees and a flat cap, almost a uniform, and his florid face sported a drooping grey moustache. She thought he looked self-righteous.

"*Bonsoir*," said Nicolas and stood to shake hands. Alexandre followed suit. Everyone understood where allegiances lay, but it was unthinkable not to be polite under these close circumstances.

"A beer, please," the newcomer demanded, and Jerome served him with a quiet disdain.

"What brings you to my door? It is a surprise," Jerome remarked. All the while he was watching Monsieur Demille and listening for the slight that he was sure would be forthcoming soon.

"I've things to tell you," replied his neighbour, looking at the two young men who were leaning against the bar. "Later," he added. "Let me drink this first. It's been a long day and I'm thirsty."

Jerome gave a small shrug. He turned to converse with Alexandre about his day's work and the weather. The visitor became agitated with the waiting.

"There are things to discuss, as I said. I spoke to *Monsieur le Maire*. We can talk here, if you prefer." Monsieur Demille looked again at the other customers. With that, the two young men decided to leave rather than become involved in this village bickering.

After they had gone, Jerome said, "Well?" This time he did not disguise his dislike.

"As I said, I have spoken to le Maire and as you well know, he represents the gendarme in this village. Your yard is a disgrace. It's filthy, and I'm sure rats are everywhere. The chickens stray. They are a danger on the road. Get it cleaned up," Demille finished in no uncertain terms.

Harriet gave Suzy a pointed look and shook her head slightly.

"If you have spoken to the mayor, then why isn't he having this conversation with me?" Jerome asked, matching the man's belligerence.

"He told me to go ahead and speak to you."

"Oh right, so he doesn't want to get involved in your foolish ramblings."

"I'm warning you…" said Monsieur Demille. "It could go badly for you and this so-called business of yours." His face grew redder and his chin wobbled with agitation.

"Don't you go threatening me," said Jerome, becoming flustered.

It could have escalated, but at that moment Éric ambled in. Harriet explained to Suzy that Jerome knew that this argument would upset the younger man; he would end up shaking and frightened.

Jerome took a deep breath and, turning back to Monsieur Demille, he said, "It's time you left now."

Heading for the door, his neighbour turned as he opened it. "Oh, by the way, the committee decided about the food for the *ducasse* tomorrow night. You may not get the contract this year!"

"What did he want?" asked Éric as the door closed behind Monsieur Demille.

"It's nothing for you to worry about, Éric. He said the chickens were out again," Jerome answered.

"What did he mean about the food for the *ducasse*?" Éric persisted.

"Again, it's not for you to worry. He was just being his usual nasty self."

Suzy caught a glimpse of an anxious expression as he turned away from Éric.

The next morning, Madame Altier, accompanied by Suzy, was heading for the post box when they passed Monsieur Demille walking in the opposite direction. Suzy waved at Jerome who was watching the street. Madame and Monsieur greeted each other with the customary set of kisses and he shook hands with Suzy.

"*Bonjour*, Madame Altier," greeted Monsieur Demille. "*Ça va?*"

"*Oui, ça va*," she responded.

"How is business?" he asked.

"Oh, not too bad for the next few weeks. I have had this English lady staying, Mademoiselle Suzanna Summers. I understand she might move over here." Madame Altier looked at Suzy before turning back to Monsieur Demille. "She is investigating the area."

"Well, we have enough houses for sale around here, but more English? We don't need more," Monsieur Demille frowned, despite Suzy standing in front of him.

She nodded politely at him and then crossed the road to hide her anger and gaze at the sunflowers pushing their way up towards the warmth. She could still hear their conversation but she pretended not to.

"So few young French do up the older properties, Monsieur. They prefer to build on available land rather than putting in the money and effort to renovate. At least the English incomers' money keeps our village going."

Monsieur Demille harrumphed and said, "They are spending their money in our local shops, I suppose, but I don't like it!" He raised his hand and spoke behind it, coughing to disguise his words as if Suzy couldn't hear. "I don't trust them."

"Maybe she could buy me out, and I can go and live with Camille." Suzy glanced over her shoulder and saw Madame Altier smile at the thought that had popped into her head.

"How is your sister?"

"She was so poorly just before Christmas, and she keeps asking me when I might sell. I don't know, though. It's my home." She paused before adding, "I warned my visitor not to go there!" Madame Altier nodded at Jerome's restaurant. As Suzy rejoined them, she saw Madame's expression sour.

"I was in there last night," Monsieur Demille said. "I told him his yard is a disgrace. I hinted he may not get the *ducasse* business this year," he added with a smirk.

"Is that so?" Madame Altier asked, leaning in closer.

Monsieur Demille tapped the side of his nose conspiratorially. "You never know."

CHAPTER 5

On returning home to England, Suzy was hardly able to contain her feelings of uncertainty, nerves and excitement. She'd spoken to Edward a few times on the phone while away. Tonight, she would explain her plans to him in full. He would be hurt, but she was sure he would accept it with good grace.

She unpacked and dressed with care. She wore the green dress that Edward liked. It brought out the colour of her eyes, he said. As she peered into the mirror to apply makeup, she understood that she did not love him and perhaps she never had.

At exactly 7.30pm, the doorbell rang. She sighed.

"Suzy." Edward beamed and enfolded her into him. "I have missed you," he mumbled into her hair. "I was going to bring flowers but I ran behind, and I knew 7.30 was approaching. I didn't want to be late."

"A few minutes here or there doesn't matter," she said as he released her.

"Shall we go? I can hear all about your little holiday on the way," he said.

Little holiday! Suzy thought indignantly. *He has no idea, even though I've explained so many times.*

They got into Edward's car and headed to a cosy Italian restaurant. While they drove, Suzy told him about the people she had met and the things she had seen. It was important to keep it general until they sat down together, and he was not concentrating on his driving.

"Ah, this is a quiet little corner. I like this restaurant," Edward said as they arrived and seated themselves.

"Edward," Suzy said quickly, wanting to get her news out, "Madame Altier, the lady I stayed with who owns the B&B, well, she wants to move out to her sister's. She's elderly and finding running the place too much for her, on her own. If it works, I could buy her out and take over the business."

"What do you mean?" Edward asked. "You would live in France?"

"Well, yes. You know I was thinking about it. Nothing has been discussed, exactly, but it's the change I need right now. It might not happen, and she might not sell, but something like that would suit me."

"I see." Edward met her gaze, his grey eyes suddenly looking a little dark and formidable.

The waiter came and they placed their orders. Suzy wished she wasn't trapped there for the meal.

"What about your work, your house?"

"Edward, dear Edward," she started, reaching across the table to take his hand. "I need to pursue this change for a while. I've been wallowing for too long, looking after Mum, working at the same place all these years."

"Seeing me and going out as we do. Stuck in a rut," he finished morosely.

"No! I just need to move forward. My life has changed with Mum's passing."

"So, it's a done deal. You've decided."

"Yes, Edward, yes I have. I need this now. If you want us to end, I understand. Maybe we should call a halt for the time being."

"I don't want us to end. I love you," he said.

"We're good friends," she said. "I hope we'll always be that."

Their first course arrived and perfidiously she was glad it was something to occupy them. She watched as Edward slowly took up his cutlery. She grabbed her fork with false vigour.

As soon as possible the next day, Suzy rang Jo.

"Hi, I need to speak with someone who is not so involved in what I am planning," she said. "Can we meet up for a coffee?"

"That sounds intriguing," Jo responded.

After work, they met at the coffee shop on the edge of town. As she parked, Suzy immediately spotted her friend's bright pink top and red curly hair, around which she'd wound a colourful scarf. She sat in a window seat waiting for Suzy, eager to find out what needed to be shared. She grinned as Suzy entered.

"Are you pregnant?" she asked. "Have you won a massive fortune on the lottery? Are you running away with someone?" She laughed.

"No, no and sort of," Suzy answered.

Jo's bright blue eyes widened. "Oh my! Tell me. I'm burning up with curiosity."

Suzy shared all the details of her recent holiday, the people she had met and her plan to go and live in France.

"So, you'd give up your job?" Jo asked incredulously.

"Yep, that's the plan," she answered.

"Do you really want to isolate yourself like that?" Jo asked.

"I'm not isolating myself. It's five hours away, max. I can come and visit quite often if I want."

"Wow! After all this time, same job, same house, same life. What about Edward?"

Suzy shrugged but said nothing.

Jo nodded. "Well, mega good luck to you! You deserve it. Can I come and stay? I may find myself a romping good

French person." She raised her eyebrows suggestively. "Did you meet anyone I could tear off into the night with?"

Suzy laughed at her friend's one-track mind.

Jo leaned forward. "Well, it's time you got on with real life, Suzy. You were seventeen, weren't you, when your dad died? You had such a lot on your plate, taking on all that responsibility for your mum. I know she always seemed frail and vulnerable. She enjoyed the finer things in life without understanding how they were funded."

"Dad dealt with mortgage payments, insurance premiums, banks and life in general. It freed her to enjoy her clubs and groups; her regular visits to the hairdresser and manicurist. Her work was being a good hostess for Dad's business colleagues and their wives. She had little idea of the practicalities of daily living."

"Everyone loved her, though," Jo said, "because she was always charming, always looked beautiful. I remember her being so polite, and she never forgot a name, a birthday or an anniversary. There's no doubt that your mum loved you to distraction. And when she lost your dad, you stepped up and took care of her. You've never been afraid to work hard, have you? Always practical and realistic ... and patient."

"It was my choice to stay and help her out and not go away to college." It was true. As she'd matured into adulthood, Suzy had worked at the head office of a finance company a short walk from her home. She'd studied and trained hard, eventually becoming a Senior Financial Adviser. She managed the accounts of the top clients, and often earned herself excellent bonuses.

"Fair enough, but now it's time for you to follow your own dream," Jo insisted.

By the time they said their goodbyes, the tonic of Jo's bright, generous personality was working its old magic, and Suzy felt much better. Her initial excitement had returned and she went home with renewed enthusiasm and walked up the path to the bungalow that was hers alone, now. She noticed with appreciation the cloud of primroses, the daffodil leaves pushing their swords through the earth and the buds on the bushes bursting with a froth of bright green.

After letting herself in, she leaned against the inside of the door for a moment before kicking off her shoes and heading for the bedroom to discard her jacket. Her head was spinning with possibilities, something that hadn't happened for a long time. She cradled her mug as she sat on the sofa and tucked her legs under her. The television was left turned off, as she stared at the empty grate and thought things through. Savings in the bank had mounted during the time she had nursed her mum and with money she could get from the sale of the bungalow, surely that would give her enough to move to France, wouldn't it?

It was getting late and her half-drunk tea had grown cold. Tomorrow she would search the internet about living in northern France and seeking out properties. Madame Altier's B&B would suit her well but that might never be for sale. It wasn't even on the market. A couple of weeks holiday wasn't the same as moving abroad permanently. Tomorrow she would take a reality check and consider everything afresh.

It took Suzy forever to get to sleep, but she was wide awake the next day. For the first time in ages, she was full of energy.

After work, Suzy made herself toast and tea before switching on her laptop. She settled in for an evening dedicated to searching the internet. There were areas of northern France that were flat and, in her view, uninspiring. This was inland from Calais and Dunkirk. Going the other way, as she had done, towards Boulogne, she had discovered the area known as the Seven Valleys. The photos were beautiful, and Suzy could not resist looking again at the places she had visited. The blueness of the sky that melted into the hazy purples of the distant hills, the meadows full of wild flowers that smelled wonderful, and the wooded hillsides were all beautiful.

Suzy was about to look again at properties for sale in the area when a knock at the door startled her. When she opened it, Jo was there.

"Twice in as many days? Come in! I've been thinking about your news."

"Guess what I've been looking at on the internet," Suzy laughed.

"I'd love to see the exact area."

The two had been friends for years, although so different in many ways. Everything about Jo was larger than life. She was tall where Suzy was not particularly, and even her hands were broad and competent looking whereas Suzy had long fine fingers.

Jo always looked extravagant in her choice of style. The colours she wore reflected her loud and warm personality. Today her red curly hair was tied with a yellow scarf which left tendrils escaping. She wore emerald-coloured jeans with a yellow and orange jumper. She lacked all self-consciousness and was the only person Suzy knew who could be so outrageous and get away with it as a result.

She folded her long legs and sat next to Suzy on the sofa so they could both see the screen.

"I was just about to look at some properties for sale," Suzy said after they had read the travel descriptions of the Seven Valleys.

She was pleasantly surprised. Although house prices had risen abroad and things had stagnated in England, she would still get more for her money than in the UK. Her mum and dad had bought their bungalow when prices were low and they'd lived there until they were mortgage free, so she would be able to afford somewhere in France. "You should get a good price for this place," Jo said, reading her thoughts.

"My needs aren't great, but I'd have to run a small car if I lived out in a country village. I'd also need enough money to feed myself." She had to be realistic.

Suzy knew that she would need to revisit the area of Fleurus-le-Comte again, and soon.

CHAPTER 6

Eager to continue with her ideas, Suzy dialled Madame Altier's number later that week. Perhaps, as Easter approached, she would be busy, but Suzy hoped she'd be able to return to the same B&B.

"*Bonsoir*," answered a distant voice.

"*Bonsoir*! Madame Altier?"

"You are Eenglish?"

"*Oui*. It's Suzy," she continued in French.

"Ah, Suzy," said Madame Altier.

Suzy managed to make herself understood. The telephone was always more difficult than a face-to-face conversation. Thankfully, the B&B had a room free for the days that she wanted.

When Suzy arrived back in Fleurus-le-Comte, the sky was grey and heavy, but her spirits were high.

Having had a good sleep, she arose with optimism and ambled along the road, taking in the sights, sounds and smells. All was becoming so familiar to her.

I must go into Jerome's restaurant and book a table, she thought. *Madame Altier will not be happy, but she'll learn that I won't be intimidated.*

Suzy pushed open the door with slight apprehension. Though often filled with men at this time of day, the bar was quiet. Jerome stood alone behind the counter as he washed glasses.

"Suzy, *bienvenue*." He flung the tea towel over his shoulder and beamed at her as he came forward and greeted her with kisses on either side. His cheeks were rough against hers.

"I wondered if I could eat here tonight?"

"Of course, it would be my honour," he responded. "Always a pleasure to have the English here."

They exchanged pleasantries but Suzy didn't want to hang around, despite his offer of coffee. "See you later," she said before she left to continue her stroll.

It took her along the little lane beside the river, towards Harriet's house. On the spur of the moment, Suzy decided to drop in on her to pursue the friendship they had begun during her previous visit.

Harriet smiled when she saw who had rung the bell. "Come in, come in. Lovely to meet you again. I've just got to finish clearing up in the studio. If I don't do it, things will go hard and be impossible to clean."

"I don't want to interrupt," Suzy said as she followed Harriet through the house.

"Not at all. Welcome to my workshop. I make pots and ornaments. I've just got a few tools to finish washing."

The space was lofty and old. An extractor fan whirred somewhere in the background and in the roof, skylights were cloudy with age and dust.

The table in the centre of the floor space bore several cloths, sponges, tools and mats, but all was laid out tidily. Next to the table stood a potter's wheel with its seat attached. In the corner sat the solid cube of a kiln.

The whole space was busy and full of Harriet's work.

"Do you sell them locally?" Suzy asked as she looked around.

"I have a stall at some of the markets and there's a craft shop in town that takes them. It's not much, but it helps me to feed myself. It gives me something to fill my time." She shrugged and smiled gently. "I have what's called a micro-enterprise here in France. It's a small business, as it sounds, but taxes and other paperwork are much easier if it's registered that way. I remember last time you were here you said you might want a place like Madame Altier's. If you run a B&B, that's the easiest thing. I imagine Madame Altier's is run that way. Ask when you need to, if you get stuck."

Suzy took in the shelves of vases, small wine cups and matching jugs that Harriet must have made. Some were glazed and others awaited that process. In a different style there were sprigs of leaves and flowers in bright colours.

"These are truly lovely," Suzy said as she found several painted sunflowers in a vase. "They're unique. You're skilful. The flowers are huge but each petal is so delicate. I love them."

Harriet turned from the sink. "I got the idea from a magazine a while ago. They sell well, especially in the summer months when tourists are here. There, that's that done." She wiped her hands and turned off the extractor fan. "Now, how are you?"

"I'm fine, just here for a long weekend. It's short notice, but I wondered if you would join me for a meal at Jerome's tonight. I've booked a table. My treat. It would be good to have company."

"How lovely. Yes, that would be great."

They sorted out the arrangements and as Suzy said her goodbyes, she realised she was excited to be strengthening their connection.

As she left the B&B later that evening, Madame Altier said, "I don't know why you want to go there."

"I'm doing research," Suzy said and gave her sweetest smile. "I need to understand what the competition is, if I end up starting a bed and breakfast like yours."

Madame Altier sniffed and turned away.

Suzy met Harriet at Jerome's front door and they entered the restaurant together.

Two young men stood at the bar drinking from the necks of the little bottles of local *Ch'ti* beer. As the women entered, they each put their bottles down and came across to say hello and give Harriet and Suzy kisses to each cheek.

"This is Suzy, remember? Alexandre, Nicolas," Harriet said, introducing the brothers again. "Suzy is interested in coming here to live, but for now she's staying with Madame Altier for the weekend."

Suzy had heard more about them from her landlady. No doubt they had heard of her too. As Suzy and Harriet sat at one end of the long table and Jerome brought them their starters, the young men returned to their beer, good manners having prevailed.

Jerome's jeans hung from his skinny hips, and he seemed to be wearing the same apron he had when she had first arrived in the village and he had given her directions. His slender frame and scruffy attire wasn't a great advert for good, home-cooked food but Suzy and Harriet fell on their meal.

"That was delicious." Suzy sat back in her chair and surveyed the room with contentment.

"I know root veg soup isn't high-end gourmet, but it's tasty," Harriet agreed.

Jerome served the main course. "*Bon appétit*," he said, before he returned to chat with the two Augustin lads. The steaks were cooked *saignant*, just as they had asked. As Suzy cut into hers, the red meat juices flowed into the pepper sauce.

"Ah, I can't believe this. Madame Altier led me to understand that things here are second rate, but this is so succulent. Jerome has done well for us here," Suzy commented.

"They don't get on, and there is envy about their respective collecting of English friends too. It must have been going on forever and a day. Apparently, they knew each other as children in school."

"Well, I shall steer the middle course and be friends with each of them," Suzy stated.

"That's what I do. It works alright and is the safest thing," Harriet said.

They were both speaking English.

"It's relaxing to speak my own language once in a while," Suzy said.

Harriet was about to answer when the door opened, and all eyes turned that way to catch sight of the newcomer.

Suzy became aware of heat rising up her neck. She tried hard to combat it with deep breathing as she realised Harriet's eyes were on her.

Jean Chri came towards them to kiss his hello. Suzy, not completely in control of her emotions, avoided eye contact. The dark stubble brushed her cheeks.

"You are enjoying your meal?"

Harriet responded for them both. He left to join the other men at the bar while Harriet and Suzy accepted their cheese course from Jerome.

There were three different pieces of cheese with a lettuce accompaniment, which had a light lemony dressing. "Normally we would have cheese after dessert or instead of it," Suzy said inconsequentially to Harriet. *Why the sudden constraint?* she thought.

"It's supposed to be better for the digestion," Harriet responded. "So, have you further plans to move here? It would be good to have an ally in the village."

Suzy explained about her mother's death and her flagging relationship with Edward. "I need a mega change to kickstart my life," she confessed.

"Maybe you'll find someone, over here," said Harriet. "I'm a great believer in fate. I'm happy enough on my own, I suppose. I miss the companionship in the evenings, but I don't kid myself. I should be lucky to find anyone else in my situation. There aren't many gay women in this region. I'd need to go to a big city, and I have no desire to do that."

Sitting back in their chairs, they relaxed. Deep, raucous laughter rose from the bar. Both Suzy and Harriet turned toward the cause of the mirth. Suzy was unsure if Jean Chri had imperceptibly raised his bottle to her in a salute.

Really, the conceit of him, she thought.

Harriet caught her eye and smiled.

Back at the B&B, Madame Altier grilled Suzy about her meal at Jerome's restaurant.

"It has been a very pleasant evening," Suzy told her, ignoring what she knew to be the crux of her questioning. Then she took pity on the old lady and said, "The food was good, but he deals with a different clientele to you. I'm sure there's room for both in this village. I shall be eating here tomorrow evening, if I may, Madame."

This calmed her hostess. "*Bien sûr*," she agreed. "It will be special, as if it were a Sunday." Then she changed the subject. "So, are you thinking of coming more permanently?"

"It is tempting, but I have no means of supporting myself. I need to find a small business similar to yours." Suzy sighed.

"There's you wanting work and here's me with too much," Madame Altier shrugged.

"Too much?" Suzy asked.

"I can't manage on my own these days. It's hard work changing beds and cooking all the time. I must ask people for help. I had to ask Jean Christophe to help me mend my door handle. I don't like to keep asking. My sister wants me to go and stay with her, but I'm not sure."

"Perhaps you need me to come and help you out. We could be a team for a while." Suzy laughed. "Now, Madame, I must get to bed. It's been a lovely day, but I'm tired."

As Suzy lay in bed, she found it hard to relax. She reflected on her evening, smiling when she remembered bits of conversation with Harriet. She supressed the memory of the closeness of Jean Christophe, and her mind meandered among the people she had met again tonight.

Suzy awoke early. Glancing at her phone to find the time, she bounced out of bed. The sun was shining again and shadows from the trees outside danced on her wall. It was her last full day, and she wanted to make the most of it.

As she stood under the shower, the conversation with Madame Altier from the previous night suddenly crashed into her head and her stomach did flips. In a rush, she could picture what she might do. She needed to find Madame.

"*Bonjour*, Madame," Suzy said as she walked into the living room half an hour later. So much was riding upon this conversation.

"Well, Suzy, this is your last full day. Have you plans? I shall miss your company. We have had a good time together, *n'est-ce pas?*"

"Madame Altier, may I speak with you?"

"Why, what is it, my dear? You look so anxious!"

Suzy took the plunge. "Last night, you said you had too much work, and I said we could be a team for a while. Would you consider that — seriously? I need work if I am to sell my house and live in France. Perhaps I could live here and do the work that you do, and you could live here and rest more."

She stopped. A silence grew and become more constrained.

I've blown it, thought Suzy.

"Suzy!" Madame said at last. "You must call me Marie, if we are to be partners."

"Really?" Suzy almost shouted. "I appeared so cheeky, so *audacieux*."

"But no!" Madame said. "It has been in my mind for a while to find help. We get on well enough, you can live and work here, and we shall work out how we share the profits. Two can live almost as cheaply as one. When I am ready, perhaps you will have sold your house in England and you can buy me out. I shall live with my sister in Rouen and all will be well. *J'ai le cul bordé de nouilles*."

Suzy did not understand this local phrase and asked for Madame Marie to repeat it, which she did. Something to do with noodles. She would look it up later.

"Madame, er … Marie," Suzy began self-consciously, "would you prefer to think about this for a while to be sure? I do not want to push you too hard."

"I feel sure all will be well, but shall we say one week from now I shall telephone you? If we both still want this, then that is good."

"That is a good suggestion," Suzy agreed.

Marie Altier stuck out her hand and Suzy took her small, bony fingers into her own and they shook.

After breakfast, Suzy escaped to her room and fell onto the bed. Had she done this? Was she mad? Would it work? She stayed like this for a time until curiosity got the better of her and she looked up the phrase Madame Marie had used. Literally, it translated as "I have the arse full of noodles."

What? Suzy thought, puzzled. With further research, she discovered what Madame Marie had meant: "I am a lucky bastard."

CHAPTER 7

As the first week back in England drew to a close, Suzy found herself awaiting Madame Marie's call with impatience. As the end of the agreed time neared, she worried that the old lady would change her mind in the cold light of day. The closer the time came, the more desperate she was to take this next step in her life. While the challenge was nerve-racking, it was also exhilarating.

At last, one week after her return, the telephone buzzed and she snatched it up.

"Suzy?" asked the disembodied voice.

"*Oui, c'est moi*," she answered. Her hands and knees were shaking. Was Madame Marie going to douse her rampaging flame of enthusiasm? "Have you changed your mind? I would understand if you have."

"No, I haven't," Madame Marie answered. "Have you? We could have an agreeable partnership. It would be a good idea to give it a time to see if we work well together. Shall we say three months on either side? It is a trial, so to speak."

It's protection for each of us, Suzy thought. *Things need to be done properly and Madame Marie is astute. Good.*

"That would suit me well," she said.

"I shall have it put in writing for you. When would you be able to start?"

Suzy realised she hadn't considered this in enough detail. She had to give notice at work and organise things for the house. She hesitated. Marie picked up on this.

"Is there a problem?"

"No, no, absolutely not," Suzy responded. "I must tell my work, that's all. It will take one month for me to complete all that here."

She walked through to the kitchen. Glancing up at the calendar on the wall, Suzy gave Marie a date for when she could return to France. Changing her whole life seemed such a weirdly casual act, accomplished with ease.

She told Marie she would await her letter with eagerness. Then she would hand in her notice at work.

A week before Suzy was due to move to France, Marie rang late one evening.

"Hello, Madame Marie." Suzy found it difficult to call her just by her first name. Madame Marie seemed more respectful somehow, given the differences in their ages.

"How are you getting on with your preparations?" Madame Marie asked.

"I'm ready," Suzy answered. "I'm just waiting to finish with my work. Is there a problem?"

"No, no, not at all," she responded with a little laugh. "I just phoned for a chat. It is a while since we saw each other. Your room here is ready. I am looking forward to having the company and the help here."

"It's exciting for me too," Suzy said.

"One of the first jobs we may do is re-paper the second bedroom. I should welcome your young opinion on a colour and style that will match the furniture but may look a little more modern."

"I would enjoy doing that."

"Many things have been happening here in a short space of time," Madame continued. "You will never guess the shock we all had when we discovered that Maryl has left poor Jean

Christophe. She has gone to her sister's house all the way over in Béthune. That's a long way away! She says she is fed up with living in a nowhere place. Pfff! Well, I ask you! Some people are never satisfied. She has a good home and a fine, hard-working husband. I don't know how she can leave all that."

Suzy was sorry to hear this. While she did not know the villagers well, they had been congenial during her stay. Well, Maryl had been a little frosty, but not overly so. Jean Christophe had been kind and funny, although conceited. She didn't wish him bad fortune, though. She imagined, in a small community like theirs, the separation would be a major talking point. She couldn't conceive how hard that must be for Jean Christophe and his family. "I imagine she will return, won't she?" Suzy asked. "Maybe she just needs some space to consider her future."

"No, no! She is making it clear to everyone that she will not return."

"Is Jean Christophe difficult to live with?" asked Suzy. "He seems pleasant enough."

"He is perfectly *agréable*. A lovely, gentle and helpful man who has a great sense of right and wrong and a good sense of humour. Maryl does not deserve such a lovely man," Madame Marie said.

She makes him sound an absolute catch, but he doesn't come across like that, Suzy thought. She made sympathetic noises, since Madame did not need an answer.

"I hope you can bring some cooking skills with you too," said Madame Marie, changing the subject. "I would like to offer a more varied menu for visitors who are staying for several days. We must cost it carefully, but sometimes we have Dutch or French visitors who might like to experience English cooking, especially those Yorkshire puddings I have heard about. They are becoming, how do you say it, a hit over here."

"Well, I can manage that," said Suzy. "I can do those quite well."

"Yes, we need to do one better than that dreadful Jerome and his so-called restaurant. You went to eat there, so you know what it is like."

"I just went to check out the competition, as I said."

"You know his restaurant is not so good, and he has that cousin living there and those young men calling all the time. His wife left too. I told you that? Now, she couldn't stand it and I don't blame her one bit. That was quite a different matter to poor Jean Christophe. I don't consider Jerome likes women. He is always quite rude to me."

A smile spread across Suzy's face. "Well, we all have to live side by side," she said in what she hoped was a conciliatory way. "I'm sure we can offer something complementary to his restaurant so that we are not catering for the same *clientèle*."

Two days later, Suzy met up with Jo again at a café in the town.

"Good to see you," she said, giving Jo a warm hug. This time, her friend wore an orange scarf in her red hair and an orange and royal blue top to match. Her full red lips were always laughing, or so it seemed. Suzy so hoped she would come out to visit and said as much.

"I will," Jo said. "Wild horses won't stop me. Now, tell me about Edward. How is he coping with all this excitement and change?"

"It *has* been difficult. I've made it clear what's happening. He was morose for a while but now he's being so kind and sweet about it all. It's hard to tell him everything. because deep down he's hoping it will all just go away and that I'll change my mind at the last minute. Every so often he asks me why I'm doing it. Poor Edward, but I want to get there so we can both start a new phase in our lives."

Suzy saw Jo's grimace. "Now, come on Jo," she continued. "You think I could have done better. Well, I agree with that now. Don't say I told you so either." She smiled. "Changing the subject, Madame Marie phoned last night." She gave Jo a rundown of their conversation.

"Ooh, I might run away into the night with this Jerome. Is he appetising?"

"Well-seasoned, but not appetising," Suzy informed her.

"Well, what about Jean Christophe, then?" Jo noted Suzy's lack of eye contact. "Ah-ha!" She rubbed her hands together and laughed. "I smell something tasty here. Spicy, is he?"

"I suppose, if you like that kind of thing. A bit obvious, in my opinion."

"We like sauce, though, don't we?" Jo winked.

Suzy shook her head, tutted at her friend and smiled. She was used to Jo's outrageous remarks. "Madame Marie has got it in for Jerome," Suzy said, changing the subject. "She is spreading rumours about him and they are sticking in high places in the village, it seems."

"She sounds a right tartar. Why on earth are you hitching your wagon to hers? She doesn't sound nice at all." Jo looked concerned.

"Her bark's worse than her bite. She's determined to undermine his business and get rid of the competition. I can stand up to her and she deflates quickly. Anyway, how about you?"

"You know me; easy come, easy go, always out for a laugh," Jo responded. The smile seemed brittle, and Suzy wondered if her friend had an upset that she hadn't shared.

"Is everything alright, Jo?" she asked. "It's been all about me, but there's something wrong, isn't there?"

"You're too sharp," Jo smiled. "I have to move out of my digs, that's all. I must find somewhere else in a hurry. It's all a pain."

"But you're sharing a house with Amy from school. You've been living together for years, and as an item for most of that time. I thought it was a good arrangement. Didn't you say her flight routines fitted well with you working from home, too?"

"Yeah, but it hasn't gone quite so smoothly in the last couple of months. Amy and I have had some serious arguments. She's started going out clubbing again. I'm through that phase. She says I'm too staid and getting old. Me! I ask you."

"Like an old married couple," Suzy ventured.

"Oh well! Such is life. Look, I'm going to have to make a move. I'm supposed to be viewing a flat in town."

"Are you moving that soon?"

"Yes, needs must and all that," she answered glumly.

"Where is this flat?" Suzy asked.

"It's above the shops halfway along the High Street. You know where I mean?"

"You have got to be joking. It'll be poky and noisy and smelling of takeaways. There will always be doors banging and loud music. You'll hate it."

"I've got to live somewhere, though. It will be cheap, so there's an upside."

"How about shacking up at mine for a few months until you've got yourself sorted? After all, it will be empty," Suzy offered.

"It would be a solution for me." Jo sighed.

"And for me! If it all works out in France, I shall sell, but not just yet."

"I'll pay you rent," Jo volunteered.

"Okay. We can sort that out. Just a peppercorn rent would do. Every penny will help me, but I wouldn't expect you to pay a going rate since you'd be helping me out."

"I couldn't afford your house on my own. Are you sure you'd be happy with an arrangement like that?"

"Of course I would. It would be helpful. It's weird how things work out, given time," she added.

"I'll call round tomorrow evening then, shall I?" Jo asked. "I better go now and kick this other thing into touch. Bless you, Suzy. You are such a good friend. By the way," she added as she stood to leave, "I should definitely visit and sort Madame out about this Jerome thing — and rescue him from the clutches of the village grandees."

"Don't you come and upset the apple cart!" Suzy laughed. "I do hope you will come over soon, though. I want to be able to talk to you once I've moved, and it will be so much better if you have seen it all."

At last, the time came for Suzy to journey into her new life. She bowled along the motorway, her car almost overloaded. She had her little television, a kettle, a giant box of teabags, bags full of clothing, framed photographs and one of her own paintings, of which she was particularly proud.

As she drove into the little village of Fleurus-le-Comte once again, Suzy felt she was arriving home. This time, the fields were dark green with maize and the buds of the sunflowers were still at the stage of turning with the sun. It wouldn't be long before their bright petals burst open to reveal the gold of her dreams.

A green tractor was in the field as she passed the village sign, cruising across the terrain and spraying. The driver, whom she at once recognised as Jean Christophe, waved at her from within the cab. She felt hot but tutted to herself. Her thoughts rambled unbidden: *I wonder what he's up to now? He's still married, though, so… His wife could return. She needs space, that's all. I'm sure she needs a break from him occasionally.*

Taking the correct turn and descending the hill, she passed other familiar landmarks. The flower troughs on the little bridge were now full of geraniums, fuchsia and begonias. She took in the burbling river; Jerome's restaurant and bar; the church with its massive, ancient tower; the *Salle des Fêtes* with the *mairie* next door and the home of Madame Marie Altier, cut into the hillside. Suzy's new home.

Suzy almost sprang out of her car and leapt up the steps. She turned to survey the village and took in an immense breath. She was here. At last. She let it out with a relaxing sigh. Within seconds, Madame Marie opened the heavy oak door and spread her arms wide to greet Suzy.

"Please, come in, my child," she said and gave Suzy an eager hug before the obligatory kisses of welcome. "How was your journey? Come and have a coffee."

"I must fetch my things and get settled."

As Suzy was taking her second load in, Éric, Jerome's cousin, appeared from down the road.

"Do you want help?" His accented French was hard to understand, but Suzy got the gist of it.

He swayed from side to side as he walked. His build was massive, and his arms were burly, though he was not tall, and Suzy was grateful for his kind offer.

He started chatting to her, but she found it hard to understand any of what he was saying since his local *Ch'ti* accent was strong. She gathered, from a few words here and there, that his conversation veered between all manner of disconnected subjects, making it almost impossible to follow. Suzy found herself nodding and smiling, taking her cues from the expressions on his face.

Some of his words were patois as well. He referred frequently to his *petit pote*. Suzy worked out he was saying his little mate, but he meant his dog. This convoluted exchange took time to negotiate, and both Éric and she were laughing a lot by the time she understood.

Madame Marie appeared at the door. "Éric, you must speak slowly for Suzy. She does not understand you. Come, come this way with those things and don't drop anything." She hustled him in.

Suzy marvelled that Éric was accepted by the old lady, but she was sure Jerome would never be allowed to cross the threshold.

Eventually, the bed was piled high with all her paraphernalia and she thanked Éric and said goodbye to him. She had no doubt that all her gear would be described in full and reported all around the neighbourhood before she could blink.

Madame Marie said, "I'll leave you to sort your things out, and I'll see you in the living room when you are ready."

It could not have been a warmer reception. Suzy was reassured that she had made the correct decision to come and undertake this change. All her anxieties floated away, and her shoulders relaxed.

CHAPTER 8

By the end of the first week, Madame Marie and Suzy had agreed on the new décor for the bedroom. They visited the DIY shop and bought paint and rolls of paper. Looking on the internet, Suzy found the best way to strip off old paper. She sprayed it before scraping with a mix of water and fabric softener, and it worked well.

"Madame Marie," she called on entering the kitchen. "Oh! There you are. I need a hand moving the wardrobe. It's too heavy for me on my own. It'll be far too much for you too."

"Éric or Jean Christophe will help, I'm sure, if I make a phone call."

Five minutes later, she appeared in the bedroom with the news that Jean Christophe would come up to help, but not until he finished milking the cows.

Okay, Suzy thought. *Well, I'm bound to bump into him from time to time. I can handle him and his conceit. No problem.*

She and Madame Marie sat at the table and had a coffee while they waited. This was how Jean Chri found them when he arrived.

"Come in, come in," Marie said.

"I heard you were coming when I met Madame Altier on her way to the graveyard with flowers," he said, looking at Suzy. "It's good to have someone new here with fresh life and interests."

"Will you take a coffee?" Marie asked.

"Shall I do the job first, Madame? Then I'd love one," he said. "Perhaps you would show me, Suzy?"

As he pronounced her name, Suzy's tummy did a swoop. *No! This won't do*, she thought as she led the way to the room being decorated. *I'm in no rush to get involved elsewhere so soon after Edward, and certainly not with a married man. His wife might return at any time.*

As he followed her down the corridor, he said, "I saw Éric helping you with your things. You were talking and laughing."

"I couldn't understand much of what he said," she laughed.

"Not many of us do, but *you* looked happy."

Suzy glanced back over her shoulder. He sounded ungracious with his statement or perhaps she had misunderstood and he was being wistful. The corridor was too dark to see his expression.

As Jean Christophe and Suzy struggled together with the large wardrobe, she noticed his hands. Hands always appealed to Suzy. Edward's were long-fingered and slim, but Jean Christophe's were broad and brown, with a fine covering of dark hair; the hands of a farmer. His fingers, strong and square-ended, had short, clean nails.

The heavy armoire was a real struggle to move. Much involuntary giggling took place as they grappled with the massive structure. Eventually, they moved it far enough away from the wall for Suzy to get behind so that she would be able to finish scraping off the old paper. By this time, they were both breathless and laughing, and ready for a rest and a cup of coffee.

Jean Christophe took a deep breath. "This coffee smells good and you have something good cooking, too. I do miss the comforts of a woman's touch. Companionship and closeness at night and well … Maryl, for all her difficulties in those directions was a good cook and homemaker. I can look after the house and cook but I have little time or patience for all that." He shrugged. "Still, I know that at certain times of the year it can be lonely as a farmer's wife."

"I think she was never satisfied." Madame Marie nodded. "You tried to provide the things she craved and we were all surprised when she left."

"I've failed," he said. "I was pushed into speaking sharply too many times. My house is not a home anymore."

Suzy sat in silence throughout this exchange.

He glanced at her. *Self-absorption will not endear me to anyone*, he thought.

"Goodness knows what some people in the village must be saying. Oh well…" As Jean Christophe prepared to leave, Madame Marie suggested he come for dinner one evening.

"It's a thank you for your help," Madame Marie said.

They settled for a few days hence.

"Suzy, show him to the door, why don't you?" Madame added mischievously.

"Thank you so much, Jean Christophe. I should not have been able to manage on my own." Suzy spoke formally as she pulled open the heavy front door.

"No problem at all," Jean Chri said. "I have only myself to please now, and so I'm available to help you, should you wish. I'll see you in a few days for dinner. I look forward to that." He smiled, revealing his white teeth, and those dark brown eyes twinkled.

Suzy used lining paper when decorating because the walls were so uneven, but she painted over it, choosing a pale cream colour. For the windows she chose fine voile curtains in bright turquoise. Nothing thicker was needed with the shutters to close at night. Against the cream it looked fresh. Madame

Marie agreed to buy a new duvet cover and pillowcases, so Suzy chose the same colour for those. When the room was finished, although the furniture remained dark and heavy, the whole effect was clean and airy. Suzy was pleased with her work.

"What a splendid change," Madame Marie enthused. "We must ask Jean Christophe to help move the armoire back against the wall when he comes for dinner, then all will be complete."

"Have we a booking for this room soon?" Suzy asked.

"Yes, at the end of next week. I will show you my bookings diary and go through all that with you. Then if you take any calls, you will know what to do and what information to gather."

Suzy was gratified that Madame Marie was happy to include her in the commercial operation. There would be bookkeeping and taxes to learn about too, in the future.

A few days later, Suzy devised a menu for their dinner with Jean Christophe. "I shall cook Yorkshire puddings to go with the main course," she said, "but other courses will be French-cum-English, because many of the things we eat are the same anyway."

"It will be pleasant not having to decide what to eat," Madame Marie said. She smiled at Suzy.

Jean Christophe was due to arrive at about six thirty. By six forty-five, Suzy wondered if he had forgotten. She was so used to the absolute punctuality of Edward. The bell at the door jangled, interrupting her reverie.

"Answer it, Suzy, please," Madame Marie shouted. "I am finishing my hair."

Suzy wiped her hands and left the kitchen to open the door. "*Bonsoir*," she said and smiled up at Jean Christophe.

"Suzy," he greeted her and leant down to kiss her cheeks. She inhaled his fragrance, clean and elemental, like rain on the grass. There was the merest hint of lemon cologne, and Suzy felt breathless once more.

Madame Marie joined them in the living room, where she poured wine and offered little snacks. "After we have relaxed here, Suzy has prepared a delicious meal for us."

"I hope it's delicious," Suzy laughed a little nervously.

"Why would it not be?" Jean Chri asked seriously, but he had a twinkle in his dark eyes.

The Yorkshire puddings were a great success and Suzy had even managed to make a trifle, having bought ordinary gelatine and flavoured it with fruit juice. This dessert was unfamiliar to the French but disappeared with speed.

"Suzy, that was good," Madame Marie said. "Oh, we must have that as a regular on our menu for our guests who stay here."

"Indeed," echoed Jean Christophe. "That was truly delicious."

"We are hoping you have enjoyed your meal enough to help us move the wardrobe back," Madame Marie cajoled, smiling across at Jean Chri. If Suzy didn't know better, she could have sworn that Marie flirted with him.

With his easy attitude and provocative looks, he seems to bring that out in people, Suzy thought.

"Of course I shall help," he said comfortably.

"Well, sit first and take coffee. I shall go and prepare it. Suzy has done enough. Stay here, you two, and chat together," she said as she disappeared.

After a few moments of silence, the conversation started. By the time Madame Marie returned they were prattling and laughing together, muddling through the language barrier with congeniality and warmth.

Much later, after struggling to move the wardrobe back and after more wine and coffee, it was time for Jean Chri to leave. The latter part of the evening melted away in a haze of cosy gossip, laughter and warmth between the three of them.

As Jean Chri ambled down the road, he gazed up at the countless stars. Considering her long glossy hair, her eyes, her slim waist, he'd been attracted to Suzy the first time they'd met, although it had not crossed his mind to take it any further. He had still been living with his wife. Now it looked as if that period of his life was over. Maryl had made that clear.

The conversation and good food he had just experienced warmed him as he walked slowly down the road. He liked Suzy's wide smile. It was so long since he had been the cause of someone's face lighting up like that. Her green eyes pierced his psyche and remained with him as he entered his own house.

Wearily, he climbed the stairs and got ready for bed. Reality hit. He was still a married man, even though his wife had departed and was not inclined to return. Suzy had mentioned someone called Edward. This was in passing and she had not gone into detail, but perhaps she had a man back in England. She might well leave this village after a while. Back where he started, he felt hopeless and a failure.

The week after the dinner at Madame Altier's passed in the normal way. The weather remained reasonable. Jean Christophe did his daily round with the cows and in between he planted sugar-beet in his fields. On top of this, he washed his clothes and managed his household in a desultory fashion. He saw Suzy once or twice and waved, and he was gratified that she returned his greeting. By the end of the week, he was tired and deflated, despite trying to maintain an air of normality.

As he entered the cowshed at about half past five on Friday, he saw a car pulling into Madame Altier's driveway. This must be the guest that was referred to. A man who looked about forty, around his own age anyway, got out of the car and stretched.

As Jean Chri looked up to the house, he saw Suzy by the front door at the top of the steps. He couldn't help but dawdle on his task so that he could watch the scene unfold.

She waved, and he heard her shout, "Edward!"

Their voices carried on the breeze. "What are you doing here? I couldn't believe it when Madame Marie said the visitor was you. She didn't put two and two together at first, and only a couple of days ago she told me your surname. Why didn't you say?"

"I thought I'd surprise you. After all, we're still friends."

As Jean Chri spied on the scene, he saw the man reach into the car and produce a bunch of flowers. He couldn't discern whether she was pleased or not. He saw her kiss the cheek of the man, once, in the English fashion, and the man placed his arm around her waist. Together they mounted the steps and disappeared indoors.

Jean Christophe continued into the cowshed and as he went, he meditated on what he had seen. No kiss on the lips, no warm hug. However, they were both English, and the English were renowned for their reserve. This did not appear to be the Suzy he was becoming familiar with, though. She seemed outgoing and full of life and warmth. He wondered for how long this Edward was visiting. Would they meet? That would be most interesting.

He answered his own question more quickly than he imagined. He was returning from his smallholding with a bucket of vegetables when he met Suzy on the bridge. She was accompanied by Edward. They stared down into the gushing river, but they weren't speaking. Jean Chri couldn't tell if it was a companionable silence.

"*Bonsoir*," he said as he prepared to pass. In the presence of Suzy with another man, he became unsure of himself and shy. He didn't lean in to kiss her hello which would have been the most natural of greetings.

"Oh, hello," Suzy responded with her broad smile. Before he moved on, she continued, "Edward, this is Jean Christophe. He owns the farm over there." She waved her arm in the general direction. "Jean Chri helped me move that huge wardrobe in your room so that I was able to decorate behind it," she explained in English.

In French, she introduced Edward to Jean Chri. They shook hands in a cordial but distant fashion, after which Edward put his hands in his pockets.

"Enjoy your stay," Jean Chri said, smiling, and Suzy translated as best she could. Edward nodded but offered nothing more, and Jean Chri made his exit.

Suzy noticed that Edward was aloof after her French friend had passed on his way. They crossed the bridge and walked on without reference to the brief meeting, until Edward said, "You seem to be settling in here … and making friends."

"Yes, I like it here, and the people are kind and welcoming," Suzy agreed, not unaware of Edward's meaning.

"I know," he nodded. "It doesn't mean I have to like it!" He resumed looking at his feet as he walked with Suzy on his arm.

Suzy said nothing to this. She understood how he felt, but she was unable to give him more.

CHAPTER 9

The end of April turned to May, and then June approached. Suzy's knowledge of the business grew, and she became confident in most of it. She learned about French micro-enterprises and the taxes and insurance which were so different. She helped Madame Marie more and more with changing beds and planning meals and cooking, sometimes for up to ten people. When the phone rang, she noted bookings in the diary.

Suzy had ideas to make the B&B business even more healthy. These she kept to herself for now. It was early days; she did not wish to appear pushy.

Since she had an afternoon off, Suzy took a stroll around the village. Things had been so busy she had spent little time doing this and so met few people. Suzy headed towards the bridge when, as she passed Jerome's door, Harriet approached.

"Hi, I'm popping in to see Jerome," she said. "If I don't go often, he thinks I've fallen out with him. I guess he's used to that with others." Shrugging, she added, "Are you coming in?"

"Yes, okay. I haven't seen him in a while either."

They entered the bar. Silence.

Harriet called, "Hello, *bonjour*, Jerome."

The old man appeared, wearing the perennial apron, and came forward to greet them with arms outspread and a wide smile.

"How good to see you both. Are you like this with me?" He touched his two index fingers together to signal a disagreement.

Harriet caught Suzy's eye. "No, never," she reassured him.

"And how are you getting on, Suzy?"

"Everything's fine so far," Suzy smiled back at him.

"I understand you may take over the business," Jerome stated. The local chatline operated well. Suzy wondered how much he knew and how much he would like to know. She told him how things stood.

"Jerome, what's happening about the food for the *ducasse*? I remember what you said about Monsieur Demille threatening to get it taken away from you." Harriet changed the subject.

"He is an old bag of hot air, *comme d'habitude*," answered Jerome. "I've got the contract, but I'm doing all I can to show them. The menu will be good."

"Any clues?" asked Harriet.

"No, not even for you!" He smiled. "It's a surprise, so that everyone will be impressed. Are you helping with the decorations again?"

"Yes, the A.E.P. committee are doing it as usual. Hey, perhaps you would help too?" She turned to Suzy. "Many hands ... and all that."

"I'd love to help, but what am I letting myself in for?"

Harriet went on to explain. "The whole village turns out for a long afternoon and evening of games, drinking, feasting and music with fireworks to finish. A group of the men put up a large marquee, or *bulle* as it's called here, for the tables and chairs. The women decorate it all."

The village did not own its own *bulle*. There was a call for some of the farmers to take a trailer across to the next village to collect one. They were to erect it too.

"There's a meeting next Tuesday evening to organise everything. Will you come along?"

"Of course," answered Suzy.

"It's in the *Salle des Fêtes* at seven thirty. Shall I come and call at your house for you, and we can go in together?"

"That would be great," said Suzy.

"Well, I must make tracks now." Harriet prepared to leave.

"Do you want some eggs?" Jerome asked. "I've got salad leaves you can have too, if you like. Would you like some, Suzy, or would Madame Misery disapprove?"

"That would be great. Thank you," she responded, ignoring the jibe.

Jerome went to fetch his offerings, and after his return Harriet left.

"Harriet is so kind," Jerome said. "A good friend. Things have not been easy for her. It took a while before she was accepted by some around here."

"I'm sure," said Suzy guardedly.

"There were a difficult couple of years for her. Valentine died and since then she has been on her own, but she joins in all the village life. The old biddies seem to accept her now. She pops in here to see us regularly."

That might not endear her to all, Suzy thought to herself. "I must go now too," she said. "Thank you for these."

"Let's hope they don't get you into trouble."

"I'll manage!" Suzy smiled back, nodding her understanding.

When she arrived back at the house, she told Madame Marie who had given her the produce.

"Hmmph!" Madame frowned. "We don't need his charity or anything from his scruffy kitchen."

"Well, these are from the garden so they'll be fine, and we can make use of them," said Suzy, heading for the fridge.

Later that day, she contacted Jo and asked her if she could come over for a visit.

"The weekend of the *ducasse* would be ideal," she said.

Jo was rapturous at the idea. Arrangements were made for her to stay at the B&B, since they had the room. The business was busy, but Madame closed that weekend so they could enjoy the *ducasse* without having to consider the needs of guests.

Harriet rang the bell on Tuesday evening, as agreed. Together, she and Suzy went to the meeting to arrange the *ducasse*. Jerome did not go, but several others were there. She already knew some: Monsieur Demille; several older ladies, who always helped with everything; Jean Christophe and his brother Pascal; and the older Augustin brother, Alexandre. One of the ladies brewed coffee and distributed it. Another, Claudine, had made biscuits.

Arrangements were made for the erection of the *bulle*, and jobs were discussed and distributed. Suzy found it difficult to follow all the quick details of the discussion. There seemed to be a long talk about something to do with drinks on offer.

Suzy smiled inwardly. Here, some people desperately needed to have their say and appear important in this small community, but Suzy found it charming, albeit amusing. Jean Chri glanced at his brother, Pascal, and then caught Suzy's eye and smiled at her. He understood her thoughts. As she lowered her gaze, pink climbed around her neck and her throat went dry.

Suzy was given the job of making the small decorations for the centre of each table with Harriet.

"We'll either ask people if we can raid their gardens, or it might be charming to have wildflowers," Harriet said as an aside to Suzy. "It might make an impression to have small flags with the village sign on to go in the vases too. People who come from other villages would see."

The hour was late when the formal part of the meeting concluded, and someone produced glasses and a couple of bottles of wine. People stood to chat and share news. Suzy found herself, with Harriet, talking to the group of older ladies.

After helping to clear up, Harriet said her goodbyes. As Suzy collected her jacket, Jean Chri approached. His brother had already left. He asked how she was getting on.

"I haven't seen you for a while," he said.

"I've been so busy," she answered. She was aware that Claudine's eyes were upon them. She had to be careful. He was a married man, and too much interest between them would be noted with ease.

They both turned towards the door and walked down the steps together. The only light came from that reflected from the spotlights on the church tower, and from the glow of the moon and stars. The ground was uneven, and Suzy trod carefully and slowly.

"Are you alright? These steps are treacherous." Jean Chri placed his hand under her elbow for support, drawing her closer. It seemed natural.

"Thanks," Suzy said huskily.

With a loud creak, the door to the *Salle* opened and light flooded down upon them. Suzy pulled away as other people arrived to descend the steps. She turned and fled, calling her goodbyes over her shoulder.

CHAPTER 10

"Hello," Suzy called. "Is anyone there?"

Jerome hurried through to the bar to find Suzy standing alone. "Do you need any help? I've got a free couple of hours before my friend arrives."

"That would be marvellous, but I don't want to get you into trouble with Madame!"

"Oh, that's okay," Suzy answered. "I'll tell her if she asks."

"Come through to the kitchen. I'm pleased to see you."

As they entered the kitchen Jerome turned to his cousin. "Éric, I need you to get the salad leaves picked and the tomatoes washed and put in the fridge. I'm busy dressing these salmon. Can you pass me the bag of lemons before you go out? Oh, and can you bring me in a few sprigs of parsley?"

Suzy could see he was very busy and could use the extra help — it was the day before the *ducasse*. He put his knife down and stood away from the table. When he breathed in to calm himself she realised he was beginning to feel better.

The next hour and a half passed pleasantly enough, with Suzy acting as sous chef. Jerome was also pleased to have a gossip. He started to tell her about his situation with Éric.

"Some people in this village wonder why Éric didn't go to live with his father when he left the army and was ill. Well, as a boy, his old man was quite cruel to him, but I'm not telling everyone that. Why should I? It's not their business, although they would like it to be."

Suzy mumbled a response as she peeled and chopped carrots.

"They don't know that his father used to lock him in the shed when he was young if Éric displeased him. Éric has told me it was dark and damp, and he could hear rodents. He was very frightened," Jerome explained.

"That must have been horrible for a sensitive little boy," Suzy agreed.

"*Absolument!* There is no way he wanted to go back there, as you can imagine. I couldn't allow it. Hélène — my wife — left with the children, so I had the space. People think I took him in for his illness payments. That's rubbish too. It costs me more to look after him," Jerome said angrily.

"Do you see your children?"

"No. They live with their mother."

"That is sad," Suzy couldn't help saying.

"I have Éric to look after," he said. "It is a shame that I have this little business and they are not here to take it on when I retire."

There was a pause when neither of them spoke, and then Jerome added gloomily, "Mind you, if members of the local *conseiller* and others who have the ear of *Monsieur le Maire* have their way, I shan't be in business much longer. They would be pleased if I closed."

Having finished her tasks, Suzy returned to the B&B. She liked the village, despite the little niggles and more major criticisms of some people. There were always disparate factions in a small community like this. However, the bigger picture was tranquillity and work that she enjoyed. Then there was Jean Chri. She squashed that thought quickly. *Don't go there, Suzy*.

She smiled as she remembered that Jo would be arriving imminently for a long weekend. She wanted to introduce her to the people with whom she was becoming so much more familiar. She couldn't contain her eagerness and was chattering to Marie about her friend.

"You may find her too exuberant," she said, thinking Madame might not approve of Jo, "but she is the kindest person and I'm sure when you get to know her, you'll like her, too."

By half past five the clock seemed to be creeping more slowly. At six fifteen Suzy was pacing between the front window and her seat at the dining table.

At last she heard a car and rushed to open the front door. "She's here!" she shouted in the general direction of Madame Marie. Suzy disappeared down the front steps and squealed with delight as Jo climbed out of her car. "Did you have a good journey? You didn't get lost, did you?"

Jo gave Suzy a huge grin and said, "Me? Lost? Well, near the end, but only a little."

They collected her bags and mounted the steps together, chatting non-stop.

"There's so much I want to show you," Suzy said. "We could go for a picnic, take books to read by the river. It's so peaceful and relaxing."

Suzy opened the door to the bedroom and light flooded the space.

"This is beautiful," Jo said and went to look out of the window onto the garden. "I see that's where you got the roses from."

"One of the Augustin brothers, Nicolas the younger one, comes in to cut the grass and tidy around once a week." Jo smiled at her friend before sitting on the bed. "This feels great." She gave a little bounce.

"Leave your bags — I want to show you round." Suzy took Jo's arm and gently pulled her to her feet.

"The house is beautiful," Jo said, admiring each room they passed through. "I adore the wood. It's so dark and aged. I suppose that's generations of handling. Such history, and all the chairs with their cotton covers are so bright and cheerful."

"Let me show you the courtyard at the back," Suzy said excitedly. "When we have guests they sometimes sit there for breakfast."

Upon arriving outside Jo gazed around. "I love all the troughs with the geraniums. It's all so…"

"French?" Suzy completed her sentence and they laughed together.

Madame Marie appeared and Suzy made the introductions.

Saturday morning dawned grey. It had rained hard during the night. This was not a disaster, since the *ducasse* meal was under a marquee. The weather would not be good for the planned games, though. Suzy awoke with the dawn chorus, which resounded at about five o'clock. As she lay in her big cosy bed, she focused on the day ahead. She felt exhilarated. When she got up, Jo was not far behind her and they enjoyed their continental breakfast at the dining table.

"It's a shame we can't eat outside in the courtyard." Suzy gazed out of the window. The sky showed pale blue here and there, between the clouds. Sure enough, by mid-morning the sun was struggling out.

Suzy had agreed to go to the *Salle des Fêtes* to help set up, and Jo was happy to go too. When they arrived, they found that the older ladies had started before them.

"Wow, here we have a veritable collective of old ladies," Jo said under her breath. "Do we call them a dither of old ladies?" She laughed.

"Definitely not that," Suzy said. "They all like to voice an opinion."

"Oh-ho! I sense a disagreement of old ladies. That's even better!"

"Jo, behave!" Suzy frowned and nudged her friend in the ribs.

The ladies came and kissed each of them in welcome. When Harriet arrived, Suzy introduced her to Jo and then they got cracking, folding napkins and arranging their table decorations — little pots of flowers. They looked good, and when they added the table confetti and flags they'd made in different shades of yellow and lilac to match the napkins and pots, it looked professional and attractive.

The Disagreement of Old Ladies made positive mutterings and nodded their collective grey heads. The newcomers sighed with relief.

"We've done it," Harriet whispered from the corner of her mouth.

Several folk buzzed around, setting up the games. For adults, the firing range attracted much attention, as well as giant darts known as *fléchettes*. The hook-a-duck in a paddling pool for younger children looked inviting, with the ducks painted different colours.

When the preparations were complete, they drifted off home to prepare themselves for the rest of the long day ahead.

"The meal's due to start at one o'clock, but I suspect it may be later. At least, that's my experience of punctuality here," Suzy explained to Jo. "I can't decide what to wear. I want to be warm if it becomes chilly later, but I want to look my best too. This is my first proper induction into the life of the whole village. I need to make a good impression."

"Not like you to be self-conscious," Jo remarked.

When Jo appeared later, she wore a dress with a lively red, purple and black print. True to form, she had used a matching scarf to tie up her bright hair. She also wore a chunky purple bead necklace, which partly covered her plunging neckline.

"There may be talk about that," Suzy said.

"Oh, good." Jo was so confident she carried it off well, and if the Disagreement of Old Ladies whispered, it would not worry her one jot.

Suzy was always more conservative than her friend, but had selected a dress in a vibrant green.

"That sets off your eyes," Jo said. "Your hair colour is so right for that shade too."

Suzy picked up a little black shrug in case it got cold later. "I can't afford to be too outrageous," she said.

"Meaning it's okay for me?" Jo asked with a broad smile.

"You're always outrageous," Suzy responded, "but you get away with it. You look great!"

"Thanks. The pair of us will knock 'em flying. They won't know what's hit them," she announced.

When they arrived back at the *Salle*, people were already milling about. *Monsieur le Maire*, Pierre le Bec, welcomed everyone and thanked the right people for their hard work. Suzy got a welcome as a newcomer who'd helped. She was gratified to be part of it. The mayor encouraged everyone to take a glass of crémant before the meal.

More arrivals did the rounds of kissing and handshakes. Suzy espied Jean Christophe as soon as he entered the field. He stood taller than his brother, Pascal, who was standing with his family. Jean Chri had rolled up the sleeves of his white shirt, accentuating the muscles of his forearms. His jeans hung from his narrow hips, and the whole effect was casual but highly attractive.

"Very tasty." Jo nodded in his direction.

Suzy glanced sideways at her. "Forget it," she said. "The old ladies are likely to pounce if they see any carry-on."

Several children skittered in and out of the crowd of adults, and Suzy saw a blonde child gaze up at her mother, who nodded. She remembered the little one was called Melodie. Her plaits bounced as she wove through to join her friend Thibault. They greeted each other in the time-honoured way.

She nudged Jo and nodded at the children.

"They're brought up from birth to greet each other as their parents do, and there's no embarrassment, even between teenagers. It amazes me."

As she drank her wine, Jean Chri and his family approached and she introduced Jo.

"You've gone pink," Jo muttered under her breath to Suzy. "I can see why. He only has eyes for you, it seems."

"Oh, Jo!" Suzy protested.

Pierre le Bec banged a table with a spoon and invited people to be seated. Jo and Suzy drifted to the *bulle* with Jean Chri's family and found themselves seated at the same table. Harriet arrived and found her place card next to Jo's. The children sat at tables of their own, and the older ones ensured the little ones settled. Melodie and Thibault sat together and were happy to be away from their parents, it seemed. They expected this and had done it before.

Jean Chri and Harriet took up the bottles of wine from the table and poured for all of them. The meal was excellent; Jerome had done himself proud. *After this, people must be more supportive of him*, Suzy thought as Jo and Harriet chattered nineteen to the dozen. Suzy turned her attention to the Rochefort family. They included Suzy in their conversation, explaining to whom they referred or the places about which they talked.

"Suzy, you go in front of me," Jean Chri said as their table was directed to fetch their first course.

He was being attentive. Suzy could not fault his manners, but still uncertainty wormed its way into her mind.

At the end of the meal, she grabbed a quick word with a busy Jerome. "That was magnificent," she said. "The salmon was so delicious, and the meat cooked to perfection. Ever so many people said good things."

"Thank you, Suzy. It has been hard work, but I wanted to prove to certain people I could do it, and do it well within the price."

"Well, you have done that for sure." She gave him a quick kiss on his cheek and couldn't help being aware that he had shaved for the occasion and put on aftershave. He was trying hard.

Games came later. Jean Chri showed Suzy how to hold the air rifle at the shooting stall. He placed his hand on her shoulder and helped to aim the barrel. His face came close to hers, and she was aware of his breath on her cheek. They laughed together as her aim went wide. He demonstrated how to do it successfully.

"Well, I shot rabbits on the farm when I was a boy," he explained. "And I still do that often, to protect the crops."

Even later still, music emanated from the *Salle* itself and younger ones started off the dancing. There was no sign of Jo and Suzy wondered where she was, but she had no fears for her, so she headed towards the little hall with the Rochefort family.

Pascal danced with Melodie, throwing his daughter up in the air and spinning her around until helpless giggles overwhelmed her. The other three adults stood clapping and laughing. Pascal then took his wife onto the floor, leaving Jean Chri and Suzy standing on their own.

"Shall we?" He raised his eyebrows in question as he extended his hand. The warmth and dryness of it sent a shiver through her. It was a fast dance, which felt safe, although the rhythm was intoxicating.

"Thank you," Suzy said.

The music changed to a French track that everyone seemed to know, and a large circle formed. Jean Chri and someone else took hold of Suzy's hands and dragged her into the ring. A man stood alone in the centre. With the music, the circle moved around him. At a change in the tempo of the tune, he grabbed a woman and together they knelt on one knee then the other. They kissed cheeks and a cheer went up from the circle. He left her on her own, and the process was repeated with her choosing a man. Everyone laughed and cheered at the appropriate time.

As it finished, an exhausted Suzy pushed her hair off her face and said, "Phew!"

"Shall we have a drink break?" Jean Chri raised his eyebrows and put his head on one side. There was still no sign of Jo, so they moved across to the bar and he bought her a glass of wine. Suzy found it impossible not to be swept along in the mood of general exuberance. They grabbed chairs outside in the fresh air and collapsed for a breather. Suzy looked up at the sky, which had darkened since they'd gone in to dance.

"With no streetlights, it's so dark. I can see millions of stars. I am so tiny and insignificant," she said.

"Not that," Jean Chri interrupted, "never that."

Suzy glanced across at him before smiling gently into the night.

They finished their drinks in companionable silence. He tilted his head in a silent question again, and she nodded with a smile. They headed back to the dancing.

Jo arrived. "Hello," she greeted them.

"Oh. Hi! Is everything okay?" Suzy asked, concerned at her friend's long absence.

"Absolutely. Mmm, very okay," she answered with an accompanying wink and a smile.

Harriet joined them too. Along with Pascal, his wife Amélie and Jean Chri, they began dancing. A call for the local folk dance rose again, and they formed the circle. Having been called into the middle by Pascal first, Suzy selected an older guy for safety. Another grey-haired man called her. She was the new attraction and a novelty with her accented French. Later still, Jean Chri danced in the middle. They moved around, smiling and laughing. The familiar tune changed tempo. Suzy's heart thumped with anticipation. Who would Jean Chri choose? The music ended. She recognised the knot in her stomach and the tightness in her throat as disappointment.

A pop and a crackle emanated from the sky.

"Come, come and see outside." Melodie arrived and pulled on her dad's hand, and they all rushed outside so as not to miss the fireworks.

"What a great day," Jo whispered to Suzy.

"I agree," Suzy replied, glancing away from the sky to see her friend's face lit by the firework that had shot up.

At that moment, Jo peeped across at Harriet standing on her other side, and a strange notion crossed Suzy's mind.

Finally, the late hour demanded that they head for home.

"Madame Marie said she would leave the back door open for us. She retired much earlier. She's been to many of these. Time to say goodnight." Suzy sighed happily. The villagers were becoming her good friends.

From chairs and cushions where they had fallen asleep, parents scooped up children. Suzy exchanged a kiss on each cheek with Pascal, Amélie, Harriet and several others. Then she and Jean Chri said their farewells. He leaned towards her and her stomach swooped. His lips were warm and dry, and he squeezed her shoulder. She caught a gentle smell of lemon-scented aftershave.

The next day, Suzy and Jo spent a couple of hours at the *Salle* helping to tidy up. When they were finished the weather was still fine, so they took Suzy's car and drove out of the village with a picnic, aiming for the spot Suzy had found before, where the rivers met and tumbled between the steep valley sides.

They travelled in silence. It seemed they both had things to contemplate, and they were tired. When they arrived, Suzy parked up and they lifted the blanket and the cool bag from the back of the car. Jo stretched, shook her head and spread the blanket. As Suzy sat, she took in the wild flowers that covered the grass before looking across at the steep-sided hills. Birds sang unseen among the ash trees that grew so profusely. After kicking off their shoes, they both collapsed and lay side by side, eyes closed against the strong sun.

"This is beautiful, just what we need today," Jo said contentedly. As they lay, she brought up Jean Chri, as Suzy had expected.

"There is nothing going on between us," Suzy stated. "Nor will there be. He's still married."

"Married? You didn't tell me that."

"Yes. His wife has left him. They say she's not coming back, but he's still married. She might return yet. Who knows? People are conservative round here. A married man carrying on with someone else, especially someone English, would not go down well. I don't need that kind of aggravation when I might well be starting to run my own business. Added to that, I am not interested."

"Not interested? You're joking! I saw you last night. Not interested, my foot." Jo wasn't having it.

"He's arrogant, conceited," Suzy maintained. "And as I said, he's married, so forget it."

CHAPTER 11

After her friend left, Suzy had plenty to reflect upon. Not least the answer to Jo's searching question about Jean Chri. Plus, the three-month probation period with Madame Marie was nearly up. She would soon need to make a firm commitment.

Later the following week, Madame Marie asked if she could have a word with Suzy. With trepidation, Suzy sat opposite her at the dining table.

"This sounds serious," Suzy said with a smile that belied her unease.

"No, no," Madame answered. "I thought I would like to go and visit my sister. She keeps asking me, and I haven't been for a long time. It's becoming more difficult to keep saying no."

"Oh!" Suzy exhaled. "I imagined you asking me to leave."

"Why on earth would you think that?" Madame Marie asked. "Have I told you your work is below standard? No. Have I suggested things are not happy here? I hope not."

"No, you haven't," Suzy said with a sigh of relief. "Not at all. It's just that my probation is coming to an end soon. I'm being silly and a little insecure."

"When I return, we shall talk about that. In the meantime you will have to look after the guests on your own. This will be the first time that the full responsibility will be yours. There is no doubt you will do well. How are you with that?"

"Oh, Madame Marie, I'll not let you down. The good name of this business will be safe with me," Suzy said.

"Well, I shall contact my sister and let her know I'll come. Would Monday suit you?"

"Absolutely. How long will you be gone?"

"It's a long way, so I should like to go for about two weeks. Would that be too much?"

"Not at all," replied Suzy. "I shall look at the bookings diary now, and if any more come in I shall note everything."

With that, she flitted to the drawer near the telephone and extracted the diary, full of excitement. This was a real chance for her to shine, and she felt confident that all would be well. When Madame Marie returned, they would discuss whether Suzy would take over the business when Marie was ready to go. It dawned on Suzy that perhaps Madame Marie had devised a little test for her, and she smiled to herself. Well, test or not, she would enjoy the challenge and rise to it.

So far, the diary only contained a couple of bookings, each for one night, but both wanted the evening meal. That would be easy to cope with.

On the day of Madame Marie's departure, Suzy took her to the station in her car and returned after a one-hour round trip, having seen the old lady off on the correct train. As she tidied up the breakfast things, the phone rang.

"*Bonjour*," she answered.

"Excuse me, do you speak English?" The voice at the other end asked with trepidation.

"Yes, I do. I am English."

"That's a relief. We wondered if you have a room for two nights. The only thing is, we have a dog. He's well-behaved, though."

"Oh, I'm sorry," Suzy answered. "We don't take dogs."

"Oh dear, I'm having such a problem. No-one seems to take dogs in your region."

"It's not a French thing to have dogs in the house," Suzy explained. "Most dogs are for hunting and if they are pets, they usually live outside in a kennel."

"Oh dear," repeated the caller. "Well, thanks anyway."

Suzy ended the call and went back to the kitchen to load the dishwasher.

A couple of hours later, another call came with the same requirement. Suzy started to repeat her answer from before, but then she stopped. "What sort of dog is it?"

"He's small and well-behaved," came the answer. "We'll bring his bed and food. He hardly ever barks. You wouldn't know he was there. We are having such trouble finding somewhere that will take him," the voice pleaded.

On the spur of the moment, Suzy made a decision. "Alright," she said. "I'll take him, but you would need to leave extra deposit in case there is damage, I'm afraid."

"That's fine, I quite understand," said the caller.

As she put the phone down, Suzy mentally crossed her fingers that all would be fine. She'd promised Madame Marie that she would not shatter the good name of the business. However, it would be worse if something was chewed up or peed upon.

The first guests to arrive, a lovely older couple, were on their way to Limoges. They complimented the house, as well as the food Suzy provided. As she waved them goodbye, she was pleased with herself. A couple of days later, she expected the couple with the well-behaved little dog.

Having prepared the room, Suzy had two hours to spare before the couple arrived. She decided to go down the road to see Jerome. Opening the door to the bar, she called, "*Bonjour*," and walked in. She became aware of footsteps.

"Suzy! How good to see you. We haven't seen you for a while. I wondered if perhaps you are like this with me." As before, he touched his two index fingers together to indicate bad feeling between two people. It seemed to be his standard response if he didn't see someone for more than a week.

"Absolutely not, Jerome," Suzy reassured him. "I've been so busy. How have things been for you since the *ducasse*?"

"Mmm, mixed," he said. "Wait while I put on a pan of water, and we'll take a coffee."

"How come it's mixed?" Suzy asked. She knew him well enough now, so she followed him into the kitchen. "The meal was such a success!"

"I took several compliments, but Monsieur Demille made a point of coming in and saying, 'Just because you've done one good meal, it doesn't mean things are going well for you.' I asked him what he meant, and he went on about Éric living here."

Éric wandered in, so Suzy kissed him hello. He'd been out in the garden, hoeing weeds from between the carrots. He glowed with warmth, but he wore a woolly hat. "It's keeping the sun off my head," he explained.

Jerome shook his head and smiled as he indicated that they should go through to the restaurant and sit down.

"Remember, you have good friends here," Suzy said.

"I do. You and Harriet are very good friends, and so kind," he said.

"Lots of people still come to eat too, French and Dutch as well as English," Suzy reminded him. She glanced across at Éric, who followed them and sat at the table. He put his head down and dozed.

"It's his medication," Jerome explained.

Suzy looked at him. *He has a lot to cope with*, she thought. "I'm afraid I can't stay long. I shall have to get back soon. Madame Marie is away, and I have visitors coming." Suzy glanced at her wristwatch.

"So, you're in charge, are you?" Jerome asked. "Is this you taking over? Will she be leaving soon?" He continued with optimism in his tone.

"Oh, I'm not sure yet," Suzy smiled in response. "There is a lot to sort out first."

"I hope so," Jerome stated with force. "That would be one less person having a go and spreading rumours about me and my business. I wouldn't compete with you, Suzy."

"No, I don't think you would. We serve different needs here."

"I've considered giving up, though," Jerome reiterated. "There is so much bickering, and I'm getting fed up with it."

"I seriously hope you don't do that," Suzy said. "The village benefits from having a business here in many ways. Now, I must go. Don't do anything impulsive," she added and leaned in to give him a kiss on his unshaven cheek.

"Wait one minute," he said, and disappeared in a hurry. When he returned, he was carrying a bag of eggs for her.

"Thank you," she smiled. "You really are kind."

As Suzy hurried back up the road, clutching her bag of eggs carefully, Jean Chri turned out of his yard in his tractor. They exchanged waves and smiles. Suzy had not seen much of him either since the *ducasse*.

She just had time to get home and place the eggs in the bowl on the worktop when she heard a knock at the door.

"Hell's bells," she said out loud to herself. "They're not here already?"

She'd planned to give the room a once-over to make sure everything was correct and then run through her menu for the evening before the guests arrived. She silently hoped the dog would behave itself as she opened the heavy front door.

As she greeted Mr and Mrs Jarvis with her hand outstretched, the dog yapped at her.

"Maisie, stop that," snapped Mrs Jarvis. "I'm so sorry. He never normally does that." The poor lady smiled apologetically.

"Come in," Suzy said, standing back and plastering a smile on her face. She so hoped this wasn't a gigantic error.

When Madame Marie returned, the house still stood, and all seemed calm and secure. Suzy collected her from the station, but in the car they both refrained from talking about how Suzy had coped. Madame Marie did not want to appear overanxious, and Suzy had not wanted to share her experience of Maisie, the dog, until the moment seemed right, so the conversation veered towards Madame's holiday with her sister, and the things they'd done together. Madame Marie had had a much better time than she'd expected. She'd been sorry to say goodbye when the time came.

Having pulled into the driveway and parked the car, Suzy carried the bags up the steps and into the hallway outside Madame's bedroom door. Then they sat at the table together to talk.

"So, tell me all," Madame said. "How did it go?"

"Everything's fine. There have been no complaints, and in fact two emails arrived that were complimentary. Actually, one of the couples brought a little dog to stay with them," Suzy stated boldly. She'd learned that to be confident with Madame Marie was always the best policy.

"What? Not in the house, surely!" The old lady's tight grey curls shook as she shuddered.

"She was small and behaved impeccably. You must come and see the room," Suzy reassured her. "I had several enquiries about whether we took dogs, and I declined all the others. Do you get many such requests?"

"I often do from the English, and sometimes from Dutch people too," Madame replied.

"We are turning a lot of business away if we refuse all the people with dogs," Suzy said.

"We'll discuss this tomorrow," Madame Marie said. "I'm too tired now."

"As you wish," Suzy agreed.

That night, she couldn't sleep. Madame Marie's reaction to changes they might make worried her. She wanted what she saw as improvements. Overhanging all this were fresh doubts about whether Madame would relinquish the reins when it came to it.

The morning dawned wet and grey. This suited Suzy's mood, weary and flagging, when she awoke. She showered and dressed and went along to the kitchen to start breakfast for the two of them. When Madame Marie arrived, Suzy gave her a tired smile.

"Are you alright, my child?" Madame Marie asked her.

"I didn't sleep too well," Suzy answered.

When breakfast was over and the table and kitchen tidied, Madame Marie said, "Shall we sit down together and talk about where we go next?"

"I'd welcome that," Suzy said.

"My sister really wants me to go and live with her," Madame started. "I haven't been sure. This has been my home for so long, and I have built up a successful business."

Suzy nodded her agreement. She sat ill at ease and leaned forwards. The tenseness crept up her back.

"Anyway, while I was there I had a chance to consider all aspects. The time has probably come for me to move there and sell up here. I will give you first refusal on buying this place because I know you will not let the business go downhill. From our brief conversation last night, I can see you have ideas, good ones, for extending it and keeping up with the times. I'm getting too old to do that."

Suzy sat, unsure of what to say.

"Is there a problem? Do you need time to think about it?" Madame Marie asked. "It is a big decision and a major change for you. I understand you need to sell your house in England. We could arrange the handover here to fit in with that."

"I should like to stay here and buy this place," said Suzy. She had wanted this for quite a while. However, now that the opportunity presented itself, she must exercise caution. She'd spent years being careful when she'd lived with her Mum. "I need to think overnight. Would that be alright?"

"Yes, of course, my dear, and if you need to visit England to discuss it with someone, Edward perhaps, you must do that."

"No, I don't need to discuss it with Edward," Suzy informed her.

Later in the day, Suzy decided to phone Jo. She needed good advice.

Jo answered the call quickly. "Hello, Suzy, is everything okay?"

"Yes, fine. How are you?"

"Your ears must have been burning. I was going to phone you."

"Oh, is everything alright with the house? Are you having problems?"

"It's not that at all. I'm coming over for a long weekend again."

"Fantastic! When? I must check we have a room free."

"Well, that's why I was going to ring you. I'm going to stay with Harriet."

CHAPTER 12

Several days passed since Suzy's call to Jo, and it was not long to wait before she drove into Fleurus-le-Comte. She had said she would call in on Suzy upon her arrival.

The great slab of stone at the front of the house had, at some time in its previous history, been part of the steps up to the door. Now it sat upon short pillars and acted as a seat. Suzy sat and relaxed with the warmth the stone absorbed. She had a book on her knee, but it went unheeded as she looked down the street. She watched out for Jo, but her eyes were lured to the long, white farmhouse of Jean Chri. She followed the gravel driveway round one end of the house to where the great barn arose. Suzy could make out the tractor in the shadows and she heard a calf but of John Chri there was no sign. *I wonder what he's doing,* she thought. *But why should I care?*

Then Jo's car approached, its wheels scrunching on the limestone chippings that covered the driveway. Suzy had a hundred and one questions for her friend. She waved and ran down the steps past the brimming troughs of bright geraniums she had placed along the low wall.

"I need to know you are not upset with me for staying with Harriet and not here," Jo said.

"I'm not! I'm surprised, but not upset."

They climbed the steps to the front door and went indoors.

"It's as simple as the fact she asked me," Jo said. "We hit it off when I came for the *ducasse*. We seem to have quite a lot in common," she added. "She's a little lonely, too."

"Yes, she's been on her own since her partner died some years ago. The house is old, and what with the garden at the back, it's all a struggle."

"Yes, she told me all about that," Jo added.

"She has her work. She works from home too, but I gather money is tight." Suzy frowned. "Anyway, come on in, and will you stay for a coffee?"

"A cup of tea would be even better," Jo said with a smile.

After general greetings with Madame Marie, who then wandered off, Jo sat at the table.

"It's great to have you here, Jo," Suzy said. "I have to ask, though, are you just good friends with Harriet?"

"We'll see," Jo responded. "We seem to get on well, and we have a lot in common. She's lost her partner and I've lost mine, albeit in different circumstances."

"Have you been in touch since the *ducasse*?"

"Mmm." She nodded.

"Well?" Suzy was impatient. "Come on, tell me."

"We've spoken on the phone ... several times. We'll see how things go. It's very early days. Don't read too much into anything. I'm just here for a visit," Jo insisted.

"Okay, okay," Suzy said, raising her hands in surrender.

"Tell me all the latest with you," Jo demanded. "The taster you gave me on the phone has whetted my appetite for all the brutal details."

Suzy took a deep breath. "Well, Madame Marie has given me first refusal on this house and business. She's ready to retire at last and move to her sister's. The other thing we discussed that I need to share with you is that she'll fit in with my timescale for selling up the bungalow. The probate's complete, which makes things easier. I'm afraid this would affect you, living in my house."

"Not a problem at all. You're giving me good notice. Anyway, I'll be on hand to show prospective buyers around if it helps."

"That's a relief," Suzy said.

"And where does Edward fit into all this?"

"Well, he doesn't. I've been through all this with him umpteen times. He needs to accept things for what they are. I hope he'll find someone else soon."

Jo looked sceptical. "Let's be realistic, he'll not take it well!"

"Well, he's been aware for ages that this has been in my mind. I've not hidden anything from him. He's refused to listen and accept it. He thinks I'm having a mid-life crisis, and all will just go away."

"I'm not sure I can picture Edward living the country life over here, anyway. He's so conservative and … English in his cord jacket." Jo grinned.

They chatted a bit more, and then Jo looked at her watch and announced that she must go. "I'll speak to Harriet. You'll come for dinner? I'll call you. We'll meet for coffee and gossip in a day or two anyway." With that she got up, gave Suzy a hug and left.

A couple of days later, Jo called on Suzy and they headed down into the village for a stroll along the river.

"I like this way best. The houses are interesting to look at on that side and there's always something to see in the fullness of the river on the other," Suzy said.

"There isn't much front garden to these houses but some of the flower boxes on their window sills are pretty," Jo said. "The water level of the river seems higher today."

"Perhaps the weir downstream, on the edge of the village, has closed a little. Apparently, it gets blocked sometimes.

Grass, reeds and silt seem to end up clogging the mechanism," Suzy informed Jo. "Several articles in the local paper have mentioned it. There's talk about removing the whole weir."

"That sounds like major work," Jo said.

"Some environmentalists seem to think it better — the river would flow more deeply and quickly. On the other hand, an action group say the strength of the banks would be reduced, or something. Other groups, the fishermen for one, don't want the weir to go either because they say they can experience different fishing above and below it. I don't understand. Plus, it's in a different language so even harder to follow but I'm trying hard."

"You sound well informed," Jo said. "You're getting into it all."

"I do read the paper. It's helping me get to grips with the language better."

They passed Harriet's little house but saw no sign of her.

"She's busy in her studio," Jo told Suzy, "which offered me the opportunity to meet you and chat."

They reached the bench beside the willow tree and sat.

"What about coming over here, to France?" suggested Suzy. "You could work from home here as easily as in the UK."

"It's tempting. I make my appointments to meet clients, say, two days each week anyway. If I timed them together, it might work," Jo answered.

"So, you have considered the idea, then," Suzy pursued.

"It's a plan," Jo said, "but only a fledgling plan. Harriet and I haven't discussed anything definite yet."

The following week, Suzy talked with Madame Marie about the possibility of converting the outhouse into a kennel for the larger dogs which might travel to the B&B with their owners. She had already agreed that one or two smaller ones might accompany their owners into their rooms. Suzy appreciated this major concession from Madame. She offered to use some of her savings for the conversion, having done research on the cost of materials.

"Who will do the work?" the old lady asked.

"I wondered if Alexandre might help," Suzy answered.

"We'll ask Jean Christophe first," Madame Marie stated. "He has more skill."

Suzy took a deep breath to calm herself. She wasn't sure she wanted Jean Christophe to be involved at such proximity. She had to agree, though, that he was probably more skilful, being older and more experienced.

"Will you go down this evening and ask him?" Madame asked Suzy with a glint in her eye.

When she judged that he had finished his day's work and had had time to wash and eat, Suzy headed down the road to Jean Christophe's house, aware of her heart beating and the heat around her neck. She knocked on the door and waited. No response. The wind rustled the leaves on the tall ash trees to the side of the house. Suzy knocked again but heard no sound from within. She experienced mixed feelings of relief and disappointment. Then Jean Christophe came striding around the corner. His face lit up as he saw her.

"Suzy, I was in the back yard and didn't hear the door at first."

"I propose…" she started and then coloured up as she realised what she'd said. He grinned down at her, making her feel even hotter.

"What can I do for you?" He chuckled at her confusion. The skin around his dark eyes crinkled, and a deep dimple appeared on his cheek.

Suzy explained the task in the most businesslike way possible. "It'll involve lining the old brick walls and ceiling to take some tiles. It's not huge or high. The flooring seems alright, and there's already a drain in the middle to help with washing."

"No problem," he said. "It's quieter now, apart from the milking. The hay is done, and it wouldn't take me long to do what you describe. Harvest won't start for a while. The barley is coming on but not ready yet, and the sunflowers not for another month."

She smiled up at him despite herself, pleased that her ideas may well come to fruition. "Would you be able to come and look and tell me whether it would work?"

"I can come now, if that's convenient?" he suggested.

They headed back up the road together, chatting inconsequentially.

"If I tell you something, will you keep it to yourself?" Suzy asked him, confident he could be trusted.

He nodded his assent.

"I might buy Madame Marie's house."

"Why, that's marvellous news," he said. "Is that a real possibility?"

"Yes. There are things to sort out first, but I'm sure it will happen."

"What about your friend Edward?"

"He doesn't like the idea." Suzy did not enlarge on her curtailed relationship with Edward.

Suddenly, Jean Christophe was quiet. "Oh," he said. The easy banter between them became constrained. "You will still be able to visit him, or he can come here?"

"We shall see," Suzy said, not confessing that she and Edward were only friends now. *What is it to him?* she thought. *He's married still. This will help to keep him at bay.*

They arrived at the house and went around to the back so that Jean Chri could look at the project. Describing what she had in mind, Suzy soon forgot the awkwardness. Jean Chri gave her some timescales and his views on prices. He suggested one or two modifications to her ideas, and they agreed what would be best.

"Will you come in for a beer or a coffee?" Suzy asked when they had finished their discussions.

"No, I'll head home now. I have an early start tomorrow," he excused himself.

He wants to escape, thought Suzy.

The building materials were delivered a few days later, and Jean Chri was coming to start the work. Suzy would be the one to hold the screws and pass them as required. When he arrived, they headed for the outhouse. Their previous awkwardness had disappeared. He was chatty and friendly. As there wasn't much space in which to work, they giggled together as he tried to manoeuvre large pieces of plasterboard into position.

They took a break and Suzy made coffee. Sitting outside, they drank together congenially.

"I am enjoying working together. It is fun and companionable. It is a long time since I did this. My wife always avoided my jobs or sharing these things."

"I gather things have not been easy," Suzy said cautiously.

"The life of a farmer's wife can be lonely at times. But she is a farmer's daughter, so she knew this before we married. I tried, truly I did. We will be separated formally. Things were never easy but just before she left, I could do nothing right." He shrugged. "Now I look back, her dissatisfaction started almost straight after we married. She was forever redoing the simplest of tasks I had completed. It made me feel useless and underconfident in turn. Many people will be surprised. I tried to pretend nothing was wrong." He hung his head and avoided her gaze.

Suzy put her hand on his arm. "I am so sorry. Perhaps she will think again and return," she said.

"Hmm."

"I too had disappointments." Suzy told him of her life with her mother. "I've had opportunities wasted. I don't want this to be another such one."

Jean Chri waited without speaking.

"Twice I was seriously in love, I thought. In my mid-twenties, Alan was the first one. We were together for eighteen months. I thought we might get married. Then he announced he was going to Kenya to grow peas and beans. He asked me to go and I wanted to be with him, but I was looking after my mum. She was hopeless without Dad. I stayed and he went without me. I shall never know if it was a bad decision."

"We can never be sure what might have been," Jean Chri said. "You said twice. What else happened?"

"Oh, that's a tale of stupidity. I was in my late twenties." She smirked at her remembered folly. "He, Freddy, was older than me by nearly ten years. Perhaps I was looking for the lost father figure — my dad died when I was seventeen. Freddy and I had such fun. He taught me a lot and I was up for all of it. We had been together for almost a year. Then I received a letter. I don't know how you say it wasn't signed."

"*Anonyme.*" He gave her the word.

She laughed. "Yes, well, the letter was *anonyme*. It told me he was married. I was devastated. I couldn't believe it and thought it was someone telling a malicious lie, but no, it was true. That destroyed so much of my trust."

"I see," Jean Chri said and nodded thoughtfully.

The next day they were making excellent progress with the project. It seemed they were making progress with each other, too. Jean Chri told Suzy how devastated he was not to have children of his own — that it was Maryl's choice — but he took immense delight in his niece, Melodie.

"She is so joyful," he said, "like a new day; full of light. And she is always giggling. It is so infectious." He talked at length and laughed at himself. "Listen to me going on."

Suzy told him of her plans for the house and the business. Jean Chri thought she was crazy to even consider dogs indoors and understood the sense of converting the outhouse into a kennel facility.

"I need to get a website created as a matter of urgency too, as soon as I have authority to do so," she told him. "It amazes me that Madame Marie has the strength of business she does without the full use of the internet to make bookings. To date she has relied upon word of mouth, previous visitors and a tiny mention via another site; the one I found when I was researching this region. I'm convinced that a designated website that details the facilities and prices would help, especially with photographs. I would link it to the main tourist websites."

Jean Chri smiled at her enthusiasm. "You have plenty of good ideas. You will make a great success of the B&B, and it will be better for the village to have a thriving business. It will help Jerome and his restaurant too."

As they neared finishing the construction work, they stood back and bumped into each other. It was the most natural thing when he put out his arms to stop her from falling over, and she leaned into him. The warmth of his hand through the thin fabric of her shirt, the smell of his aftershave, made her gasp and she looked up at him. His eyes were gentle and his expression serious.

"Whoops, sorry." She tried to laugh.

CHAPTER 13

Jo stayed for two weeks. During that time, Suzy could see a growing friendship between her friend and Harriet. She had been to Harriet's for dinner and witnessed Jo's ease at the house, almost as if it were her own. She fetched things from the kitchen, helped with the dishes and seemed comfortable.

Suzy had intercepted an exchange of looks between Jo and Harriet during various conversations; looks that suggested more than just a platonic friendship. If their relationship did progress, Suzy would be very happy for them both.

The announcement for the village *brocante* and barbeque arrived in the post about two weeks after Jo departed. The *brocante* would commence at 7am and the road would be closed off for the stalls.

"I'm amazed it starts so early," Suzy said to Madame Marie. "I know all the other villages have a *brocante* at this time of year. Do they all start at that time?"

"This is the normal course of events," Madame Marie explained. "Anyone can man a stall, and many of the villagers use it to get money for unwanted items. You know Madame Charpentier, the lady with the little twin boys? Well, she washes, irons, and folds all their clothes when they've grown out of them. She keeps all the boxes their shoes come in and has a stall to sell them each year. She makes quite a tidy little sum. The next sets of clothes are funded that way. Experienced dealers from further afield come, too. They are here early to buy, and sometimes they sell interesting things."

"Do you go and buy or sell?" Suzy asked.

"Sometimes I've had a stall, but I don't buy. I've enough rubbish of my own without buying someone else's," Madame said.

"I see there's a barbeque and a drinks tent too," Suzy said, having read the rest of the pamphlet.

"Sometimes it's pleasant to sit in the shade and take a beer or a glass of wine. It's a time to meet up with friends and exchange news." Madame Marie smiled at Suzy's excitement.

"Do you know if we have guests that day?" Suzy asked.

"Yes, but they don't arrive until late afternoon," Madame responded.

At six o'clock on the morning of the *brocante*, Suzy slowly became aware of clattering in the street outside the house. She staggered out of bed, dragged her fingers through her hair and peered down at the road. Sure enough, Marc, with his perennial roll-up hanging from his mouth, stood watching the proceedings. As the village *bricoleur*, or handyman, he looked after the verges and cut the grass at the *Salle des Fêtes*. Now he lifted metal barriers off a trailer and placed them across to shut the road. Small stripes in white paint were placed at regular intervals all down the street to mark the size of the pitches. Sellers arrived to set up tables, unloading weird and wonderful things from white vans and car boots.

Suzy showered and dressed. The weather was fair but at this hour still chilly, so she wore a cardigan with her cut-off jeans and pink checked shirt. By mid-morning, the living areas of the B&B were tidy and the beds were made. She fastened her sandals and was ready to go exploring the stalls.

"I've done the room for the people arriving this afternoon," she called to Madame Marie. "Do you want to come down with me?"

"No, you go ahead," answered the old lady. "I might wander down in a bit. Have fun, but don't go bringing back any old junk." She chuckled.

Suzy wandered down the street and nodded a greeting to several people with whom she was now familiar. A waft of fried onions tickled her nose. Apart from that, the air was fresh with a light breeze and she felt content. She looked over all the stalls. A lot of sets of china or glasses were incomplete. Odd chairs and books in French were piled high. One stall was selling old postcards and photographs. She looked in the section for Fleurus-le-Comte, and to her surprise she found a picture of her house. She grinned at the lady behind the stall.

"*Ma maison*," she said, waving the card. The picture showed the house in faded sepia and white, and there was writing on the back. Suzy read aloud: "*La Poste, Fleurus-le-Comte.*"

The stallholder beamed at her and nodded.

Suzy paid for the card. She had probably been fleeced, but she couldn't get over the fact that her house had been the post office for the village and beyond.

Halfway down the street, she realised she had referred to the B&B as *her* house. This made her feel pleased — she belonged here; this was her home. With these thoughts in her mind, she bumped into Harriet.

"Hi," she said, leaning in to kiss Harriet's cheeks. She shared her find and her excitement, then the two of them wandered on past the stalls.

"I gather you and Jo spent a good few days together," Suzy said.

"We had great fun. She's so lively and such easy company. We find we have more and more in common. Did she say she's coming again soon?"

Suzy was surprised. "No, she didn't, but then she doesn't need to check everything with me. I'm sure we'll talk soon. Have you phoned her?"

"She rang me after she left, so it's my turn. But I haven't called yet, as I don't want to appear pushy. Do you think it would be alright to phone soon?"

"Yes, of course. If you don't, she may think you don't care."

"Yes, I can see that. I wanted to, but I didn't want her to think I was being desperate."

"Just ring her. Take it from me, she will be pleased to hear from you."

They arrived outside the *Salle des Fêtes* and decided to go and sit for a drink. Tables were set up with chairs and large umbrellas, under which pools of shade tempted tired people. The barbeque had started. Several people under the shelter of a canvas tent cut bread rolls, turned sausages or burgers and fried onions.

"Oh, look, there's Pascal and Amélie," said Harriet as they arrived. "Madame Marie is sitting there too. Shall we go across and join them?"

The usual round of greetings took place and Harriet went to buy drinks.

"Where's Melodie?" asked Suzy.

"She's just gone off to play with her friend, Thibault. Oh, there she is." Amélie pointed her out.

Suzy looked across and saw Melodie giggling. "It's so safe here for children to go and have fun without the adults hovering over them every minute," Suzy said.

"Oh yes, nothing will happen in this quiet place," Amélie agreed.

Harriet returned with their refreshments, and they spent a comfortable hour together. The weather warmed up and Suzy took off her cardigan and rolled up her shirt sleeves. Whether it was the sun or the cool local French beer she wasn't sure, but she became increasingly peaceful.

"Where's Jean Chri today?" she asked casually.

"He said he'll be here later. He won't miss this," Amélie said. "It's a chance to have a lazy day. He loves spending time with Melodie too. It's such a shame he never had children. He's so good with them all, but with her in particular." Then she changed the subject. "I gather you had a successful few days. You are good for him. He's coming out of his shell. He spoke so enthusiastically, telling us about your building work."

"Really?" Suzy was surprised.

"Oh yes, he was full of it. Pascal and I noticed a difference in him," Amélie smiled.

Just then, Madame Marie turned and Suzy thought she winked.

The group broke up and everyone headed home for lunch, agreeing that they would meet up later.

It wasn't until about eight thirty in the evening that Suzy caught up with the others at the *Salle* again. By this time the barbeque was in full swing, music played, and beer and wine flowed. The atmosphere was very different to that of the *ducasse*. It was informal and noisy, with people moving from table to table and greeting friends. Straight away Suzy saw her group of friends and joined them.

"Is Madame Marie coming?" Harriet asked.

"No." Suzy smiled. "This is too lively for her these days. She will be in bed soon."

"What about your guests?"

"They're here somewhere," Suzy said. "They have a key, so they can get into their room when they want. So, I'm a free agent for a while."

"What can I get you to drink, Suzy?" Jean Chri asked.

"A white wine, thank you. I'll come with you and help to carry." Suzy headed to the bar with him.

As the evening wore on, she relaxed. Was it the wine? She wasn't sure, but she started to feel reckless. When Jean Chri asked her to dance as the light faded and the stars showed, she accepted. On the short, dry grass, the stomping turned to swaying as the music changed. His arms around her were firm, and his height made her feel safe while giving her a frisson of excitement she had not experienced in a long time. Was that his lips on her hair? She couldn't be sure at first. When she glanced up at him, he smiled so tenderly that she became more certain.

She became aware of one or two people looking in her direction and talking together. Monsieur Demille was there with his wife and Claudine, who ran every event in the village, including the church gatherings.

Suzy went on to dance with Pascal, then as a group with several others. *That'll show them*, she thought. *There's nothing going on.*

Finally, people drifted home. Few were left.

"Let me walk you up the road, Suzy," Jean Chri said.

She shrugged and nodded. She could handle him, and she was immune to any serious advances.

As they left the circle of light, he took her hand and she let him. They reached the shadows of her driveway. With care, he pulled her to one side and, encircling her shoulders with his arms, he hugged her to him. Was that her heart thumping, or his? He nuzzled her neck; he kissed her hairline and she heard a soft groan. Then, tilting her chin with a tender hand, he leaned his head down and his warm lips touched hers. Her stomach swooped.

Gentle at first, his mouth became harder and his tongue explored her lips, her teeth and her tongue. She responded for several seconds, but then pulled away. "I'm sorry, I shouldn't be doing this. I don't want this."

"Why not?" he asked.

"You're still married. You're conceited. I don't need this involvement." Her voice shook with emotion, and she sounded cruel as her panic rose. She stepped back, swallowed hard and lowered her head.

"Oh, Suzy!" he said breathlessly. "Tell me you are feeling something of what I am. I've never in my life experienced this. Never before."

He put out his hand to hold her arm, but she pulled away, out of his reach.

"I have to go. I must. Oh, Jean Chri … I'm so … I'm not doing this," she said and fled up the steps.

CHAPTER 14

The next morning, somehow Suzy fed the guests and saw them on their way.

When Madame Marie arrived in the kitchen, she took one look at Suzy and saw that something was wrong. "Whatever is the matter, my child?"

"I can't say, I can't," Suzy responded with her head down.

"Has someone said or done something wrong? It can be sorted out, I'm sure," Madame Marie said kindly. "Sometimes people say things that they do not mean, when they have a drink inside them. This place is full of people who speak before they think."

"No, no! It's nothing like that," Suzy reassured her and gave a wan smile. "It's me. I'm getting into a situation I can't handle. It's getting too complicated."

"There is never a situation that cannot be fixed, given a little time for contemplation and conversation," Madame said. She paused. "If it's to do with affairs of the heart, sometimes it can help to talk."

Tears of worry, guilt and exhaustion came to the corners of Suzy's eyes. "Madame Marie, you are so kind," she said in a shaky voice. She reached out and gave the old lady a hug.

"Now, now, you run along and wash your face. Take courage. All will sort itself, given a little time," Madame nodded. "I am old enough to know this to be true."

Two days later, Suzy was still ashamed and guilt-ridden. She had not been out because she did not want to bump into Jean Chri. From the window she had glimpsed him going about his farm work. She wondered what the village was saying about her. She couldn't bear to be considered frivolous or shallow.

Suzy threw herself into cleaning and tidying, and she was still doing this when the phone rang. Drying her hands on a cloth, she hurried to answer it. Madame Marie was outside, pegging up washing.

"Hello," came a feeble voice at the other end.

"Yes? Hello, this is the house of Madame Altier," Suzy answered in her best French accent.

"Hello, is that you, Marie?" came the voice again.

"No, it's not Marie, but I'll fetch her for you." She put the phone down and hurried outside to call the old lady.

When Madame Marie picked up the phone, she asked who it was. "Oh, Camille," she said. "It was Suzy who answered the phone. How are you? Oh dear!"

At this point Suzy moved away, not wishing to pry.

After her call, Madame Marie hunted Suzy out and said, "That was my sister. She's on her own and not at all well."

"Oh, I'm sorry to hear that." Suzy was concerned by the worry etched on Madame Marie's face. "Is it very serious?"

"It's not life-threatening, but it sounds as though she's very ill. She has a high temperature and is coughing badly. There is no-one else to take care of her. Good neighbours are around, but it's not the same is it? She's a little frightened of being on her own at such a time. There's only the two of us; we have no other family."

"What would you like to do?" Suzy asked. "I can run this place if you need to go. I'll be fine, and I can take you to the station again."

"If I go, I could speak to the doctor, but I could nurse her too. I should like to go," Madame Marie said. "Are you sure you will be alright?"

"Truly, I shall be fine," Suzy reassured her friend. "I'm sure there are people I can call upon if I'm in a fix."

"Yes, right," Madame said vaguely. "I'll go and pack a bag. I still have time to catch a train this afternoon."

The following day, Madame Marie rang Suzy from her sister's house in Rouen.

"Camille has a horrid touch of bronchitis — bad luck at this time of year."

"I'm glad you went," Suzy said.

"Yes, she's two years older, and it's scary to be on your own when you're ill and getting on in years. I'll look after her. I'll administer medication and make sure she eats. How are you? We don't have many reservations for guests at the moment, so it's quiet."

"I'm okay. How long will you need to stay?" Suzy tried to sound reassuring.

"I'll be back in a week to ten days."

Amélie knocked on Jean Chri's door, which stood open to the evening air. Her basket was over her arm, empty and ready for eggs.

As Jean Chri came through to the kitchen to answer, she gasped, her mission forgotten. He looked bleak and exhausted.

"What on earth is the matter? Are you unwell?"

"No, I'm not sleeping well," he answered. "Come in."

He put a pan of water on the stove to heat. The range was not lit. The evening was warm enough without it, but Amélie understood it provided hot water for the bathroom too.

"You'll take a cup of coffee?"

"Mmm," she responded. "Jean Chri, what *is* the matter?"

He looked around and sighed. Pots in the sink waited to be washed. Letters and unattended forms lay on the table. There was an open newspaper left on the chair next to the wood burner. The house was scruffier than ever before.

"I've made a fool of myself." He shrugged and avoided her eyes.

"With Suzy?" She was perceptive enough to gather how things had been going.

Jean Chri nodded. "She was hurt in a big way by someone who was married, and I overstepped the mark and scared her."

Amélie looked at him with a piercing gaze.

"I know. I'm unwashed and unshaven," he said. "I put on an air of confidence when Maryl left. Suzy believes I am conceited. She looked at me with contempt."

Amélie hugged him. "Right, I will visit her. Tomorrow, while you are out at work and after Melodie has gone to the *école maternelle*, I shall come and tidy up here. Now, get the range lit, heat the water and run a good bath or shower."

Amélie brooked no argument. Kissing Jean Chri on both cheeks, she hurried away.

As Suzy finished the call with Madame Marie and put the phone back, there was a knock at the door. She had a moment of panic as she went to answer it. What if it was Jean Chri? She wouldn't trust herself not to cry.

Suzy opened the door and peered around. Amélie stood on the step. Suzy sighed with relief, but in the next breath worry returned. She was concerned that this new friend would be cross and may have lost all respect for her.

Amélie smiled. "*Bonjour*, Suzy. *Ça va?*"

"*Oui, ça va*," Suzy responded. "I am well, but … I've been better."

She held the door wide for Amélie to enter. They kissed each other's cheeks.

"Please, come through." They went to the dining area. Suzy hurried to the kitchen and put on the coffee machine, eager for Amélie to know she was welcome. She would be devastated to lose this friendship and for Amélie to think worse than Suzy did of herself.

"What's wrong, Suzy? If you don't want to tell me I shall accept that, but you are not happy, and Jean Chri is far from contented again. In fact, I did not even see him like this when Maryl left. Back then he worked hard and was quiet, but now he seems to be in despair. I have never seen this before. Is there something I can say? Can I help in any way?"

"Oh, Amélie," Suzy said, and it gushed out. Suzy told her of her previous relationships; her feelings for Jean Chri and her desperation for acceptance in the village. Despite her resolve, she cried. Tears of guilt and sadness enfolded her. This was the one thing she did not want to do but she was exhausted and tense. Everything was so dreadful.

Amélie came around the table and put her arms around Suzy's shoulders. "*Chérie*," she said gently. "Do not weep. Why don't you tell this to Jean Chri? He thinks you do not want him."

"I can't see him," Suzy groaned. "I can't hurt Jean Chri further. I gave him the wrong impression. He is not as arrogant as he has led me to believe. I understand that now. But he is still married, and I cannot change that. Maryl may change her mind yet. I cannot lose the respect of the people who live here."

"I understand." Amélie nodded. After a few seconds, she sighed and added, "Remember, you cannot recover the moment after it is missed. Be careful, *ma chérie* Suzy."

She left after that. Suzy, alone in the quiet, empty house, sat with her thoughts. Panicking, she paced and couldn't settle. She felt the need to do something, but wasn't sure what.

Then, she grabbed her jacket and keys. Banging the heavy front door behind her, she took flight down the steps. With her head dropping, she passed the farm and ran for Harriet's house. She couldn't get there soon enough and left the gate swinging as she thumped on Harriet's front door. Harriet answered quickly.

"Harriet, I'm so sorry but I must go. I must leave. Is there any chance you might sort out the guests for me for the next week? It's a case of letting them in and changing beds. Perhaps Jerome can feed them if they're booked for an evening meal. I'm sorry to ask. It's important. I should be so very grateful," Suzy gabbled.

"If you have an emergency, I'll do what I can," Harriet said calmly. "Shall I come up now? You can show me what dates you have."

"Thank you, Harriet. That's marvellous. I'm so grateful," Suzy said again, humbled in the face of such generosity.

"What's the problem?" Harriet asked as they trotted up the lane together.

"I can't stay. I must get back to England. I've made a huge mistake and Madame Marie is away," Suzy stuttered, embarrassed. "Jerome might do the meals for you," she repeated.

"I'm sure he will, but Madame Altier may not appreciate that," Harriet stated.

"She won't be happy with me about any of this, but I just have to go," Suzy said with increasing panic.

"Okay, okay," Harriet soothed. "We'll manage fine, and we'll sort out Madame. I won't ask the details; that's not my business. If you must go that badly, then go. I've been in some sticky spots myself in the past."

Suzy sorted everything out with Harriet as best she could and packed her bag.

"You are coming back, aren't you?" Harriet asked, frowning.

"I have no idea what I'm doing, but Madame Marie said she'd be back next week." Suzy looked into the impassive grey eyes of her friend and said, "Harriet, I…"

"Don't say anything," Harriet said. "What is meant to be will be. Jo is coming over in a few days, so you will be able to stay in your bungalow by yourself. That will help, I'm sure. She can work from here almost as easily, so she can stay for as long as she likes."

"That's good news. I am pleased for you," Suzy said. "I'll phone Madame Marie when I get back to England." She gave Harriet a watery smile and turned to go.

Suzy phoned Jo from the Channel Tunnel terminal to let her know she would have company. Jo was laid back about that but could not believe Suzy had fled in a panic.

"You're always so self-disciplined. You never get this agitated," she observed. "Have you spoken to Madame Marie?"

"She's away because her sister is ill." Suzy told Jo of the arrangements she had made. "I'll telephone her tonight."

Jo whistled. "Good luck with that one. Don't worry, I'll be here to pick up the pieces after you've told her. Now, drive with great care. It'll work out right — whatever's meant to be and all that."

Arriving back at the bungalow, Suzy was exhausted. The rain had been thrashing down since she had left Fleurus-le-Comte.

She dragged her stuff indoors and greeted Jo, who was waiting for her with a cup of tea, followed by wine.

They talked well into the night.

"You are slightly mad for taking flight. I always said you should dump Edward for someone less tedious. Now this opportunity has arisen, and you've run away."

Morning came grey and heavy. Suzy awoke with a cracking headache. She still hadn't rung Madame Marie and knew she must do it, that minute. No more prevaricating.

Suzy picked up the phone with trepidation and dialled the number Madame had left for her. When she got through, Suzy explained what she had done, and that Harriet had agreed to look after everything.

"Oh, my child, *quelle un pétrin*. At least Harriet is trustworthy. She will manage, and I shall be home again in a week or so."

"I'm so, so sorry," Suzy said as tears sprung yet again.

"Sort it out and come back as soon as you can. I can wait. Camille could always return there with me."

"Thank you so much. *Au revoir*," Suzy managed between gulps.

Jo stood in the doorway as she finished the call. "Well, she might be an old bag, but she has a good heart buried in there somewhere. Mind you, she wants it all to be right so you can go back, and she can escape." Jo came into the room and gathered Suzy up in a hug. "Now, I'm supposed to be going to stay with Harriet again in a few days, but I can stay here if you like."

"No, you go. I shall be fine. I need to decide what to do."

Suzy met Edward briefly. She had rung him to tell him she was home. Otherwise, someone would tell him, or she'd bump into him. It seemed fair.

At 7.30pm the next evening, the doorbell rang. Jo let her answer it, but she gave her a sideways look and raised her eyebrows as Suzy left the sitting room.

Edward was standing on the doorstep with a bunch of flowers.

"They are lovely," Suzy said as she took the flowers and leaned towards him to kiss a welcome.

"Suzy, I can't believe it's you, home again." He hugged her and patted her back in an awkward, avuncular way.

Suzy poured herself a glass of Sauvignon Blanc and they went through to the sitting room. Jo had retreated to her bedroom.

"I can't stay long," he said. "Maureen Dawlish asked me to go to a trustees' meeting for the local village hall. I can't miss it. She feels my skills in finance may be of use to them. So, what's happening?"

"I wanted to come home for a bit," Suzy answered.

"Well, you should never isolate yourself from all that is familiar," he said. "I didn't understand it in the first place. You're home now, though."

Suzy was evasive about her time in France, and Edward did not ask too much. *It scares him*, Suzy thought. *He thinks I might have gone bohemian on him.*

"What will you do now? You gave up your job. That was reckless," he said.

"Mmm, probably. I'll use more of my savings while I decide what to do, I suppose."

"I might be able to pull strings to get you back in," Edward said. "Let's see what I can do. Look, I must leave. Still, you've got this thing out of your system now!"

Suzy did not contradict Edward's view of her return; she had no energy. She knew she had made the right decision to end it with him.

She looked at the rain again and let out a breath. "Mmm." She mumbled her response, looking at her hands in her lap.

"Right, come here." Edward rose and stretched out his arms. She went to him and fitted where she always had, with her head against his shoulder. He put his arms around her. "I'll see you soon. I'm not sure when, because I told my friend Jean I'd go and help clean out the village hall early next weekend." He looked sheepish.

"That's fine. I've things to catch up with. We are each going our own way, aren't we? But I'm glad we can still be friends," Suzy said.

"Shall I ask about work for you when I go in on Monday?"

"Um, er, yes, you could ask." Suzy was caught off guard. "Bye, Edward."

A week later, Jo had left for France and Suzy was back in an old routine of sorts. She wasn't working, and so was living as frugally as possible. During this period, Edward phoned her.

"Mr Hackett will see you on Thursday about some work. It's a temporary contract, but he thinks he might make it permanent in two or three months."

Suzy was aware that her money was dwindling, and she wasn't thinking straight. "Thanks, Edward. I'll call him."

She pondered her situation. She felt restless. It didn't commit her to anything to go and talk with Mr Hackett. After all, she could always say no to any job offer. It would give her time to decide what she needed to do.

CHAPTER 15

Jean Christophe was on the way to his vegetable plot when he bumped into Harriet and Jo. He heard that Suzy had fled and was devastated.

"That's all my fault," he said. He ran a hand through his hair, leaving it more tousled than before.

"Surely not! How could that be?" Harriet asked.

"I must have intimidated her when I trespassed. It wasn't my right. Madame Altier is away too, so what is happening to the business? *Merde*! I've caused so much trouble."

"Suzy has gone to sort out some stuff and have space. Don't despair, Jean Chri." Harriet tried to sound consoling, but she had little idea of what was going on. "I am looking after the guests for Madame Altier, so there's no problem there. She is due back from visiting her sister next week. I can manage until she returns. Between you and me, Jerome is looking after the dinner side of things for one or two guests, too." She smiled.

"That might set the cat among the pigeons, but the village will get entertainment from the fallout." Jo winked at Jean Chri, lightening his mood a little.

He smiled faintly. "*Merci*. Perhaps if you are in touch with Suzy, you might tell her I'm sorry," he said to them both. "I would, but I am sure she does not wish me to call anyway."

That evening, he drove along the little lane beside the river to see his brother, Pascal, and his sister-in-law, Amélie. Melodie ran to him with her arms wide and her smile even wider.

"*Mon oncle, bonsoir!*" she squealed.

He picked her up and swung her round. He held her in his strong, brown arms and kissed the top of her blonde head. She smelled of shampoo and soap. Whatever befell, he would always have time for Melodie.

"*Bonsoir*, little one," he smiled at her and gently placed her down again.

"Come on, Melodie, say goodnight. It's time for bed," Amélie said, taking her hand.

The rounds of kisses and good wishes were made, and Jean Chri was left alone with his brother.

"Oh, little brother," Pascal said. He knew why Jean Chri had appeared at his door. He had gathered from the rampant rumour running around the village that Suzy had left in a hurry, and he had put two and two together.

"Pascal, what have I done? I thought she liked me too, but it turns out I was out of line. She was hurt by someone married, and now I've frightened her too and she's gone. Goodness knows what Madame Altier will say. I will be blamed for messing up all her plans, and rightly so." Jean Chri paced around and looked wretched.

Amélie returned, having tucked Melodie into bed. "Jean Chri," she said, touching his arm. "I saw Suzy before she left, and she was miserable with guilt about hurting you. She's frightened because you are still married and worried, too, about what people here will say. She doesn't want to upset local folk when she is trying to fit in and take over from Madame Altier, so she's gone to clear her head. I'm sure she will return. Why don't you ring her?"

"She won't want me to contact her since she ran from here, from me! She has another life and I didn't think it was so important to her, but I was wrong," Jean Chri said.

"Come and take a coffee," Amélie said. They sat around the kitchen table and Pascal turned off the television.

"It seems we shall never be together, but I know she is the one for me," Jean Chri stated. "She has an inner beauty. You can see this. It is betrayed by her smile. She has resilience as well. I have never felt like this about anyone. *Zut*! What a nightmare." He put his head in his hands.

The next time Jo phoned Suzy she relayed what Harriet had told her. "It will soon be *Quatorze Juillet*, or *La Fête Nationale*. The English call it Bastille Day, but the French never do, apparently. It is almost as if they wish to forget that. When the storming of the prison occurred on that day in 1789, only seven inmates were released and none of them with any serious political significance."

"It was supposed to be an infamous place, though, wasn't it?" Suzy asked.

"So they say. Anyway, the following year the *Fête de la Fédération* was celebrated when a short-lived constitutional monarchy formed. The date was adopted for a day of national celebration in 1879 in honour of the French Republic, so there's no surprise that the French don't like the title the English give."

"You're a veritable walking history book these days," Suzy said. "I didn't know half of that."

"I didn't before, but Valentine corrected Harriet once, before she made a public *faux-pas*," Jo explained.

"The village has yet another excuse for drinking, feasting and having a day off work." Suzy ached with her desire to be there.

"So long as it's not on a Sunday. You probably know that. The actual day is always the day celebrated. None of this moving it to the nearest Monday, as the English would. There'll be a drinks tent and a barbeque, and there'll be fireworks later. Before all that, *Monsieur le Maire* will present a book to each school-aged child in recognition of all their hard work during the year. It's a charming tradition, and all the children look forward to it."

Jo told Suzy that she and Harriet decided to go and collect Jean Chri and insist that he accompany them for the afternoon and evening.

"I bet he won't come otherwise," Jo guessed.

"Let me know what the evening is like," Suzy said with wistfulness.

When Jean Chri answered the door, he said, "Oh no, I don't want to go," in response to their request that he go with them for a drink at least.

"No excuses," Jo argued.

"I'm not staying late," Jean Chri stated.

"A drink and letting your hair down will do you good," Harriet said.

"Alright, harvesting has been delayed by all this rain, so I'll come and take one beer," he said.

Jo and Harriet linked arms with Jean Chri as they strode forth to the *Salle des Fêtes*.

Jo got the first round in and Harriet the second, which meant that Jean Chri was honour-bound to buy another round before he left. The weather was cool but not wet, so everyone kept their jackets on and sat at tables outside. At four o'clock the Maire started the presentation to the children. By this time, Jean Chri's brother and family had joined them.

Melodie received a picture book, with which she ran back to the group of adults and demanded, "*Mon Oncle* Jean Chri, will you read this?"

He had relaxed since having a couple of beers, and was delighted to haul her up onto his knee and open the pages. He read the story for her with great exuberance and acting, much to the amusement of the others.

Pascal and Amélie did not stay late, preferring to get home and put Melodie to bed. However, Jean Chri stayed on with Harriet and Jo. He had forgotten that one beer was all he would have.

The evening turned lively, with music and more eating and drinking. Jean Chri talked about recent events and became melancholy again, so Jo hauled him up on to his feet.

"Come on, Jean Chri, I need to move. Let's dance," she said in a merry voice. Harriet joined them on the grass in front of the sound system, and Jo began a conga with him between them. It wasn't long before others joined them, and the line of dancers got longer as it wove between tables and around the field. Beers and dancing progressed, and the evening came to a close with the three of them doing a can-can, much to the horror of the older community, including the Disagreement of Old Ladies. Jean Chri was only half aware of glances and shocked comments directed at the English.

"Hi, Suzy," Jo spoke into the phone.

"Oh, Jo, how are you and how are things there?" Suzy asked wistfully.

"You missed a great evening yesterday," Jo said with enthusiasm. "Harriet and I went to the *Quatorze Juillet* celebration, like I said, and guess who we got to come along with us!"

"I suspect you are about to tell me." Suzy almost laughed at the earnestness of her good friend.

"Only the man himself," Jo told her ecstatically. "I told you we'd call for him."

Jo told Suzy in detail about their evening, about Jean Chri's unhappiness and how they'd got him to forget his sorrows, at least for the evening. When she related their final dance session and the response of the group of older ladies, Suzy was a little mortified.

"I hope you haven't given all of us a bad name, Jo."

"Mmm, I may have done. Sorry! They are too stuffy though," she added. "Harriet will make it right, I'm sure. They like her. Anyway, how are you and other lover getting on?"

"I'm *not* back in that old routine," Suzy answered. "I am wondering if Edward has met someone, though. He's very cagey about things. Oh, and I've got a sort of interview. It's a temporary position but I'll see how it goes."

"You're not coming back in a hurry, then?" Jo asked with surprise in her voice.

"I don't know, Jo. To be honest, I'm not sure what to do. I'm so sorry to have let Madame Marie down. She rang me and told me she hoped I would be back soon. How can I do that and not keep bumping into Jean Chri?"

"Okay, so he's married, but these are modern times, Suzy," Jo stated.

"The village is such a traditional place. That's what I liked about it. People will turn against me, and Maryl may come back. Then what would I do? I should lose everything. I wish I'd been there yesterday, though. It sounded like such fun. Instead I was stuck here feeling sorry for myself."

"Get this thinking phase over with soon, Suzy," Jo said. "Time wasted is never recovered."

With these words echoing back and forth in her mind, Suzy finished the call. She was left feeling down and turbulent.

At the end of the week following the national celebration, Jean Chri received a phone call from Madame Marie asking if he might come and collect her from the station, since she understood Suzy was still away.

"This is not a problem for me at all," he reassured her.

"I will bring my sister, Camille, with me," she said. "She's much better but still weak, so with Suzy away and Harriet looking after things, it would be best if I come back and bring Camille."

"That sounds like the best thing," Jean Chri concurred.

At the appointed time he met the two elderly ladies, and after carrying their bags he helped one and then the other into the back of the car. Madame Marie was chatty on the way home, but after a few comments and bits of conversation Camille dozed for the rest of the journey. On arrival he helped them with their things and at Madame Marie's insistence he left them inside the front door.

"Who's that in the kitchen?" Madame Marie said to herself. "Harriet must be here. I understood the last guests went early this morning, and we weren't expecting anyone else for a while. Maybe Harriet has accepted another booking." She shrugged.

"I don't know, Madame." Jean Chri waited to ensure all was well.

"*Bonjour, je suis de retour*," Madame shouted her arrival. There was no reply, and nobody came forth. Madame Marie went through the living room and into the kitchen. The noise indicated she was clearly unprepared for the sight that met her eyes.

Camille looked at Jean Chri and he shrugged, wondering what was going on. She took off her coat and as she made her way through the living room after her sister, she laid it across the back of a chair. She jumped as her sister shouted, "How dare you come into my house, into my kitchen! What are you doing?"

Jerome must not have heard the ladies' return and when the door opened, Jean Chri saw he was drying the last of the pots. "I've been assisting with the cooking," he stuttered in confusion. "It wasn't my idea, but it has been a help, I'm sure."

"I don't want you touching anything. What do you mean, snaking your way in here and sabotaging my business the minute my back is turned? Get out!" Madame screamed.

Camille was speechless to see Marie in such a state. She had seen her temper before, when they were children, but never had she seen her so red-faced and beside herself with rage.

Jean Chri beckoned him out and Jerome decided that to leave, without saying more, was the safer option. He dropped the tea towel and scuttled out. Jean Chri followed him as he hurried along. It was all Jerome could do to put one leg in front of the other. He shook so much, he did not stop. Keeping his head down, he waved a hand in Jean Chri's general direction.

"I must go back and appear normal for Éric's benefit. If my cousin sees me in this state, he will be panic-stricken." He hurried on past his own front door to find a place to hide until he had calmed himself. He scuttled along the lane, passing Harriet's little house until he came to the bench that Suzy had discovered so many weeks before. Plonking himself down upon it, he was still shaking.

"Are you alright my friend?" Jean Chri stood looking down at Jerome.

"Yes, yes. Leave me for a while." Jean Chri watched for a moment before leaving and hurrying back to see if Madame Marie and her sister were alright.

Back at the house, Camille perched on the edge of a chair in the living room and gripped the edge of the table, her bony knuckles showing white. Looking up as Jean Chri pushed open the door, they listened to the banging of saucepans, clattering of metal dishes and Marie chuntering to herself.

As Jean Chri entered his barn, his thoughts were gloomy. The humour of the village was falling apart, he reflected. His marriage was now non-existent; the woman he loved to distraction was gone; Jerome, he guessed, had become a pariah and he himself, well… He considered his brother Pascal and his family. Melodie's beaming face came to his mind, and he couldn't help but give a small smile. Thank goodness for family.

CHAPTER 16

Suzy found a skirt suit hanging in her wardrobe. She hadn't worn it for several months, but it still fitted. *If I'm going for this interview today, I better at least try to look the part*, she thought. *I'm not sure about it at all, but it was very kind of Edward to go to the trouble to get me this opportunity with Bob Hackett.*

Arriving at the office, she ran into the loo to give her hair a quick comb through before approaching Rachel at the front desk.

"Hi, Rachel, good to see you again. I've got an appointment with Bob Hackett."

"Hello, Suzy, it's been a long time," the receptionist commented. "If you'd like to go up, you know the way at least."

As Suzy rode the escalator, she wondered what she was doing there. She needed the money, but what about all the stress she'd been so pleased to leave behind just a few months ago? Bob Hackett emerged from his office. Since they had worked together for a long time, he approached her and kissed one of her cheeks, taking her hands at the same time. Then he invited Suzy to sit and took his place behind his desk, so that at least there was a semblance of formality. In reality, they just chatted about the work and he said he would be in touch.

That evening, Suzy sat wondering what to do. Her mind wandered to Madame Marie, and she imagined her changing beds, cooking meals for six or more, then sitting afterwards with a glass of wine. She missed the cantankerous, kind-hearted old lady.

Her mind wandered to Jerome. Such an old gossip, but his heart was in the right place. Despite what people said, he had not taken Éric in just so he could access his disability pay. *He's always willing to help me out and seems to thrive on being needed*, she thought.

Her mind wandered to Jean Chri and she sighed.

Just then, her mobile phone rang and she jumped. She pressed the button to take the call and her heart thumped when she realised who was at the other end.

"'Ello, *bonsoir*, Suzy, is that you?" She heard the French in a recognisable voice and realised that in her fright and surprise she uttered not a single word. "'Ello, Suzy, are you there, please? 'Ave I the correct number?" The voice struggled with a few English words.

"Jean Chri," she muttered. She was dumbfounded. "You were in my thoughts," she said after a moment's silence.

"You were thinking of me?" he asked in French.

"Well, not just you, all the people I met and made friends with in France," Suzy said, rising from her seat in her agitation.

"Oh, I see," he said and sounded forlorn. "Suzy, the reason I rang…"

"How did you get my number?" Suzy interrupted him.

"I asked and asked before Jo gave it to me," he confessed. "She didn't want to, but I kept bothering her. You mustn't be cross with her. Suzy, the reason I rang…"

"I shall have words with her when I see her. She…"

"Suzy, *ma* Suzette, *mon coeur*, be quiet, please," Jean Chri said forcefully. "I should tell you some things."

"What things?" Suzy asked weakly. He had given her a chosen name and called her his heart.

"Suzy, I understand that you had a terrible experience before we met, over there in England. Remember when we did up the outhouse for the kennel? And before you left this place, you said I am conceited. You are frightened Maryl might return and people here will be unkind because I am married still."

"Yes, I remember," she said, pacing the floor.

"Our divorce has started. Maryl will not return. *Ma chérie* Suzette, I must tell you these things or I have not done everything I can, and I should regret that all my life. I tried to be strong and leave you to make up your own mind, but you are more important to me than anyone I have known. You have strength and compassion. I saw this in your dealings with Madame Altier and with Jerome. You have a good sense of humour and … I love your eyes," he finished.

"Oh, Jean Chri. I'm sure I am not all these things. I can be as mean as the next person, and I wasn't brave when I ran away from the village," she protested.

"Please consider coming back here. Consider Fleurus-le-Comte as your home. Decide to come home to me," he pleaded. "I cannot say more, Suzy, except that I love you. I will protect you. We will be strong enough together." He allowed no time for her to answer before he added, "Please consider with care, Suzy. I must go now."

The line went dead. Suzy collapsed onto the sofa. It had taken much for him to phone her in this way and to be so honest.

"Oh my," she said to the wall. "I've so much to decide. Procrastination is no longer an option. For years, I've been here thinking with my head and not my heart and now I'm single and unhappy." *Perhaps I should listen to my heart*, she thought.

Suzy waited until Friday lunchtime. She rang Edward at work, when she was sure he would not be with a client but taking a break. They arranged that he would come round that evening but they would not go out.

At 7.30pm, she saw him walking up the path as she peeked out of the window. Whatever happened she had to speak to Edward first. It would not be easy, and she wasn't looking forward to it at all.

They greeted each other as usual, and he came into the sitting room. He made no move to sit.

"Edward…"

"Suzy…" he said simultaneously.

"You go first," she said.

"Well… It's not working, is it? There's something I have to say." He took a deep breath. "We have come to the end of our relationship. Maureen Dawlish and I are good friends. Nothing has occurred between us, but we are becoming closer. You've been away such a lot." He shrugged. "Suzy, I don't want to deceive you because I respect you too much for that. I'm truly sorry if I've shocked you. Now, what did you want to say?"

A host of thoughts blazed through Suzy's mind, but she let Edward maintain his rigid dignity. "Nothing, Edward, nothing at all. I understand it's been awkward. I've been difficult to be with, and I don't blame you for finding friendship and comfort elsewhere. Now, do you want a drink before you go?" She turned abruptly, feeling lighter than she had for several weeks.

"No, I'll be getting off now. Will you be alright? Do you want me to ring anyone to come and keep you company?"

"I'll be fine." She kissed his cheek before moving towards the front door.

It was a new day in so many ways. It was hot and sunny, for a start. Suzy could not believe it after so many rainy days. Jo rang her and they spoke for ages. Suzy told her about her phone call from Jean Chri and then about the conversation with Edward the previous night. In her own way, Jo was supportive and helpful. She was coming home in a couple of days.

"I have so much to tell you," she said.

"Tell me the juicy bits now, then," Suzy cajoled, but Jo was having none of it.

They talked more about various people in the village, and Suzy was certain where she wished to be.

"When you return, I'm afraid we need to talk about selling this house," she told Jo.

"No problem," Jo said and Suzy was relieved.

The next couple of days seemed to disappear in a whirl. Jo arrived home, telling Suzy what she planned. She intended to return to France at some point. Suzy waited impatiently until she'd had time to unpack. When she reappeared, they settled in the sitting room with a bottle of chilled Pouilly-Fumé from the Loire.

"Well, come on, then," Jo said greedily. "I take it you are going back to France."

"Yes, I am," Suzy responded with a smile. "At least, I hope I am." She grimaced. "What if I've ballsed it up and they don't want me? What if they are all fed up with the way I behaved? Oh, Jo!"

"Don't worry, it'll be fine. Everyone is being sympathetic to Jean Chri. Madame Marie is just waiting for you to return."

"What about Jerome? You said on the phone there had been a screaming match between him and Madame Marie when she found out he'd been providing the guests with meals. I was so hoping she need never find out. That was such bad luck."

"He didn't do any shouting. As far as I can gather it was all her, shrieking like a banshee. His name's mud, though."

"Poor bloke. I shall have some patching up to do when I return." Suzy sighed guiltily. "So, what about you? What are your plans?"

"Ah, well! I've got something to tell you too."

"Don't keep me in suspense, then. Out with it," Suzy demanded.

"Me and Harriet are a match made in heaven."

"So, you two got it together?"

"Yep. We have." Jo's red curls bobbed about as she nodded and laughed at the expression on Suzy's face.

"So now you and Harriet are... Well, I wondered if it was going to work out that way."

"Yep. I am so blessed."

"Oh, Jo," Suzy said. "I am so happy for you. What will you do? Are you moving over there too?"

She nodded. Were those tears in her eyes? *How perfect that would be*, thought Suzy.

"Well, here's to Fleurus-le-Comte, then," Jo said.

"And to new beginnings," Suzy added, and they clinked glasses.

That night, Suzy sent a text to Jean Chri: *I'm coming home.*

CHAPTER 17

Suzy's phone rang at half past six the following morning. She was slow to wake and had a small headache after the bottle of wine the previous evening. Surfacing, she answered the phone just to stop the noise.

"'Ello, Suzy. Is this true? Are you coming back? I didn't get your message last night. I was out until the early hours with the harvest while the weather is good. When I returned, I just showered and fell into bed. I read it this morning."

The picture in Suzy's head of him showering was almost too much, but she managed to respond. "Yes, it's true. Do you still want me to be there, though?"

"You really do not need to ask that. All that I said before is true. I'm impatient to see you again. When will you come, Suzette, *ma chérie?*"

"I have to see the estate agent, and there are one or two other things that I must do."

"Please come soon," he said. He told her again that he loved her. She felt almost new, and it was easy to respond likewise.

Later, Suzy phoned Madame Marie and said she could come back within the month. "Madame Marie, does our arrangement still stand?"

"I certainly hope so, my child." She sounded pleased to hear the news of Suzy's return, and Suzy was intensely relieved. "Camille is still here with me," Madame continued. "We shall need to decide together when you are ready to take over here completely, and then she and I can return to live at her house in Rouen. Now I am ready for that when you are, Suzy."

Jo finally wandered into the kitchen with her dressing gown hanging open and her pyjamas looking rumpled. She and Suzy looked at each other and grinned ruefully. It had been some time since they'd had a session like the previous night and lived to regret the feeling the next morning.

"I think strong tea and toast is in order," Jo said.

Having made their breakfast, they slumped on the sofa to eat.

Feeling awkward, Suzy said, "I think I've wasted Bob Hackett's time."

"No you haven't," Jo said emphatically. "He might have gained far more experience than he was prepared to pay for, so it was worth a punt for him." Then she sang, "Isn't life grand in a most mysterious way," in a discordant voice. "Don't worry about old Bob Hackett. There are far better things to think about," she added blithely.

"I suppose I'd better stop putting it off and make the call then," Suzy said reluctantly.

"Yes, otherwise it becomes one of those elephant in the corner things," she said, waving her arm vaguely in that direction as she left the room with a hop and a skip.

Suzy picked up her phone and scrolled through the menu to find the correct number. She got Bob's efficient secretary who insisted on putting her through to him instead of letting her get away with leaving a message.

They passed the time of day with meaningless pleasantries, and then Suzy got to the nub of her call. She found it was surprisingly easy. He had almost expected her to decline his offer.

"I have to work all the hours there are at the moment," Jean Chri said during one of their daily calls. "While the weather is this hot, I must get the harvest in. This is the life of a farmer, Suzy. Tell me you can really bear it. It can be very lonely, you know."

"I am used to loneliness," she said. "It will not be the same kind of loneliness with you, though, because I can look forward to the end of each day and to night times."

"This is very true." He laughed. "We shall have each other. We shall do so much with our time together."

She imagined his wicked look and the twinkle in his eyes.

"You missed a little drama recently," he told her. "Before we had this hot spell, we had so much rain. In fact, we had a mini flood. All the water washed great amounts of sand and silt from the fields and carried it down the hill into the village. A couple of us took the sweepers on our tractors to try and clear it. I think much went down the storm drains, so I hope it hasn't blocked them further along. After the rains stopped, the silt set like concrete on the road edges."

"Did it seep into anyone's home?"

"No, no. Some of the cellar pumps were working overtime in the houses along the river there, but that's not too unusual when the water table is slightly high. It was fine," he explained. "Come soon, Suzy. I miss you so much."

Suzy felt comfortable telling him she loved him, and they ended their call.

She told Jo what she'd heard about the mini flood and asked her about Harriet's house.

"I completely forgot to tell you. Yes, it was quite exciting. The water was knee-deep in the centre of the village at one point, but it went again quite quickly," Jo explained. "It has left a mess along the roads, though. Apparently when the river is high, Harriet's cellar has water in it but the pump deals with it. All the houses along there are the same, but people still use their cellars for wine and vegetable preserves and stuff on shelves halfway up the walls."

"I'm glad my house is on a hill," Suzy said.

"It really can't be a problem," Jo said blithely. "The residents of Fleurus-le-Comte know a little more about the way they live than we do since they've been there considerably longer."

Later that week, Suzy headed to the estate agent's office to put her house up for sale. She gave a little skip as she thought about her mission.

She entered the shop and the agent said he would come out the next day to see the property, and they would take it from there.

When he arrived, he immediately oozed positivity. After he had seen round the house and garden, he told Suzy some of the phrases he would like to use.

"A rare opportunity to purchase this spacious and well-proportioned three-bedroom detached... This represents an excellent purchase for a family or someone looking for quiet and spacious living... The list of benefits this property has to offer is endless... The well maintained garden will be heavenly on those long summer days... The close proximity to the station and amenities are just some of the reasons this family home will not be on the market for long, so don't delay your appointment to view this truly outstanding property, etcetera, etcetera. How does that sound?"

It all sounded wonderful and when he told her the price he thought she would achieve, she was pleasantly surprised. However, she wanted a quick sale so they agreed something that he said should do the trick.

When he had left, Suzy and Jo collapsed onto the sofa.

"I hope he sells my house soon," Suzy said with feeling. "I really want to buy Madame Marie out and get on with life, now."

"What about the sexy farmer? Surely it's not going to be like it has been with Edward; only seeing him at weekends and living separately?" Jo asked.

"Definitely not! We shall need to be careful at first, because it's such a conservative area and people could be upset about it. Maryl seems to have no real friends in the village, but people love to talk. We are going to be a full-time item but when I move in with him, at least I shall have my own occupation and income. I can't sit at home and twiddle my thumbs all day. When are you planning to move over there, Jo?"

"I was going to chat to you about that. Maybe the week after next? I have one or two client appointments to fulfil, but after that I can work from France just as easily and come back to England to see people when I need to. Harriet is fine with all that."

"It seems to be working out for both of us." Suzy squeezed her hand affectionately.

Soon after, anxious to restart her new life in Fleurus-le-Comte, Suzy decided to pack up what she needed and make arrangements to leave.

"I don't want any of the furniture. I'll get a house clearance firm in and have done with it," she said to Jo. "I'm going to put post-it notes on one or two items I might consider keeping, but there is very little. I've already got the photos and pictures I want. Do you want anything, Jo?"

Jo cast about but eventually said there was nothing.

The agent sent some people to look around very promptly, even before the paperwork was published.

"We do really like it," the first couple said. "We still need to sell our house. Would you take an offer under those circumstances?"

Suzy told them she would consider an offer but would not take the house off the market for them. The second man was going to get his pregnant wife to come and have a look. He thought it would be just right for them and their growing family, even though it was a bungalow.

Suzy was ready to go and she said *au revoir* to Jo, arranging to see her very soon in Fleurus-le-Comte. The car journey was reminiscent of that first trip she had made all those months ago. In her head, she played over and over the anticipated reunion with Jean Chri.

She knew the route so, as her mind wandered, she bowled along merrily, and the time passed quickly enough.

Coming down the steep hill into the village, there was no green tractor in the fields this time. That was disappointing, but Suzy knew Jean Chri could not stop for anything. He would be out in a field somewhere else. The stubble was gleaming, and on the other side of the road the sunflower heads were lustrous as they rippled in the warm breeze. The scene took her breath away and she had to stop the car for several minutes to take it all in.

When Suzy cruised over the little bridge and past all the familiar houses and landmarks, there was not a soul to be seen. As she slowed down and peered over her shoulder into the farmyard, she suddenly spotted the large green tractor. With a pounding heart, she swung the car round and drove through the entrance. Leaping out of the car and banging the door shut, she ran around the house to the kitchen door at the back. It stood open to allow the breeze to dispel the sultriness.

She stepped out of the searing heat into the cool interior and had a moment to take in all that was there. She loved this room. It could be the epitome of a loving family space. The floor was made of flagged slate and above her head were huge, dense oak beams.

At one end of the room was a massive fireplace in which sat a large wood burner, now swept empty, of course, but the smoky wooden lintel had large hooks that would have been for hanging hams. Either side of the fire were a couple of large chairs with wicker seats and cushions in bright colours. A cat was sleeping on one.

There was a large, dark wooden dresser upon which was all the crockery. The sink was stone, and there was a huge stove that looked like an Aga. However, there was also a newer electric cooker that was considerably more modern.

Apart from the two cushions, there was little colour in the room and Suzy fleetingly thought that she could add a rug and some checked cotton curtains. Then she heard footsteps approaching from the long hallway.

Her heart thumped and then he was there, framed in the doorway, his shoulders almost touching each side and his head stooping slightly to enter. His shirt was partly untucked from jeans that hung low and hugged his hips. Suzy could see his chest, brown and broad. As he straightened up, he saw her and their eyes locked.

"Suzy!"

He strode forwards and enfolded her in his arms. Then he tilted her chin up and his lips met hers. After her momentary surprise at finding herself with him at last, she kissed him back. His tongue probed, gently at first and with a delicacy that nearly moved her to tears. It teased her until she felt she would melt.

"At last," he murmured against her ear.

She thought her knees would buckle, but then he took her hand and led her into the hallway. In the close darkness he kissed her again, with none of his previous restraint.

"Suzette…" His voice was rasping, and he was breathing quickly.

He fumbled with the poppers on her blouse. She managed the buttons of his shirt, pulling it free from his jeans. She couldn't see his tanned chest, but she felt his muscles and the fine hair of his torso.

The next couple of hours disappeared in a blur of warmth and arms, lips and legs. His lovemaking was profound, vigorous and consuming. The tidal wave Suzy experienced was like nothing before. It engulfed her and when the internal pulsation was over, she realised it was a first-time experience for her.

After, he held her tight. "You are truly beautiful," he said, and, in that moment, she felt that she was.

They both suddenly realised the time.

"I have fifteen hectares of barley to cut, so I must go," Jean Chri said reluctantly.

"And if Madame Marie has spotted my car, which is quite likely, she will be thinking I am never going to arrive at her house," Suzy echoed his reluctance.

CHAPTER 18

As she unpacked her things, Suzy's old room looked like home again. She put out the extra photos she had brought and the ornaments on the dressing table.

Madame Marie had said to join her and her sister, Camille, for a glass of wine before dinner, and so she headed for the living room.

They were already seated at the table as Suzy entered.

"I can tell you are sisters. You look so similar," she said.

Since she had not met Camille before, both old ladies staggered to their feet and they all went through the kissing regime.

"Welcome home, Suzy," Madame Marie said. "I'm afraid there is no time to rest. Remember, I said on the phone, tomorrow we have a French family of five staying, and an English couple as well. They all want an evening meal."

Suzy smiled at Madame. "*Bah oui*! It is what I want," she said simply. "Nothing like getting straight on with things."

Suzy looked around at the now familiar scene with all the ancient knick-knacks that she had noticed upon her initial arrival. She wondered how many of these things Madame Marie would want to take. *It would be a shame if they all went*, she thought. *Perhaps we can come to an arrangement. Surely, she will not need to take all the furniture. It adds to the charm and character that attracted me in the first place, and guests love it.*

They chatted for a little while, and then Madame Marie finally asked the question Suzy felt sure had been on her mind since she'd rung the bell.

"Was that your car I saw in the farmyard across the way?"

"Yes, it was," Suzy said. Out of mischievousness, she said nothing more and waited.

"Is he well?" Madame asked, and of course Suzy knew she meant Jean Chri.

"I went to see him first because he has been telephoning me in England, and I him. We had much to talk about," Suzy told her a little vaguely.

All of a sudden, she had become self-conscious and uncertain about whether their relationship would be accepted. She certainly did not tell the two old ladies what they had been up to following her arrival. As Suzy remembered their passion, she felt herself going pink, so she rose quickly to fetch a glass of water.

"Oh, I see." Madame Marie nodded. There was a pause and Suzy quaked. "Good luck to you both, then. He deserves a little happiness."

She let out her breath and relaxed her shoulders.

"Some may be a little upset, though," Camille added. "He is still married, after all. You must be careful, Suzy. Some might take exception to an English woman taking the place of Maryl. I know from Marie she did not really have friends here, but some people may be unhappy with it all."

Suzy turned and nodded humbly. She was sure Camille was correct. They already packaged all the English together in their minds, and they had not hesitated to condemn Jo for her outgoing behaviour. Time would tell what they thought about Jo moving in with Harriet.

The next few days were a whirl of activity, changing beds and cooking for visitors. Jean Chri and Suzy had a few snatched moments upstairs in his farmhouse, but he was still working very long hours, as was she. Sometimes they had simply shared a coffee break and been comfortable together.

The children of the French family who came to stay at the B&B were delightful and the English couple, who were older, were very appreciative, saying they would recommend them to their friends. Since Suzy had been away Madame Marie hadn't accepted any visitors with dogs, even though the kennel Jean Chri and Suzy had created was fully functioning. Suzy was not really surprised. However, she accepted a booking from a couple who wanted to bring their pet.

"It's extra income, and I'm sure it will all be fine," she said to Madame Marie. "There is nowhere else offering this service, and I think it will be a good money earner."

The real focus of her thoughts, though, was on Jo's imminent arrival. She would go to Harriet's, but Suzy was sure they would meet up within the next few days. She had gathered from Madame Marie that Jo's name was still a shade of dark grey if not quite black following the dance debacle of the *Quatorze Juillet* celebration that Suzy had missed.

"It really was a bit too much for some people," Madame Marie said. "Monsieur Demille was telling me all about it. I think he is not so keen on the English at the moment. So be careful, Suzy," she advised her. "He can be tetchy."

The words pot and kettle sprang to mind, but Suzy accepted her well-meant warning.

Suzy had not seen Jerome since she'd come back but was conscious of the fact that he may think she was having nothing more to do with him, following the argument with Madame Marie about which Jo had informed her. Although she did not know the details, she knew that things had gone horribly wrong and she felt responsible.

She had sent him two postcards while she was in England, and she had thanked him profusely for his help. Feeling guilty, she determined that she would call at his house.

"Pff!" This was all Madame Marie said when Suzy told her she was going to visit Jerome.

"I want to give him a little gift because I know I caused trouble, but he was only trying to help me. I'm not sure what to give him, though."

After scouting around and thinking hard, she remembered she had a little store of English food that she had been saving for a special occasion. She arranged the pot of marmalade, the Stilton cheese, a bottle of Worcester sauce (the French seemed to like it), some decorated cupcakes she had just made and one or two other bits in a little basket on top of some tissue paper. She tied a ribbon around to make a small gift. It wasn't much, but she hoped he would like it.

She marched down the road, determined to mend any broken fences with him, but his door was locked. That was most unusual.

Perhaps he's out. I hope he's not ill or anything worse, she thought.

When ringing the bell and knocking, out of the corner of her eye she saw the drapes at the window twitch, and she was sure that it was Éric who had spotted her. As she waited, she wondered what was going on. She was standing there for such a long time that she started to fret that he was not going to open the door.

After what seemed an age, there was the sound of bolts being drawn on the inside of the door and then Jerome's face peered round, looking pale and tired.

"Jerome, are you alright?" Suzy asked.

"Please, come in." He stood back for her to squeeze around the door before he closed and re-locked it. He kissed her on both cheeks. "So, you are not like this with me?" He touched his two index fingers together.

"Jerome, I have brought you this." Suzy indicated the basket of goods that she had tried to make presentable. It looked a little puny now, although she knew he would not expect anything sumptuous.

"That is so kind," he said and gave her a hug and kissed the top of her head. "You have made it look so pretty and delicious. You do not need to buy me gifts, though. It is too much."

"It is small. You are a good friend to me." Then she rushed on. "Jerome, I am so sorry that Madame Marie shouted at you as I have heard she did."

"That? Oh, that was a storm in a teacup. I have known her for more years than I care to remember. We were at school together, for goodness' sake. She has a temper, I know that. I was shocked at the time, but that is past." He spoke with equanimity and Suzy believed him.

"You seem upset, though. What has happened? What is the matter?"

He gave the most enormous sigh and glanced across at the door to the kitchen. Getting up from the seat into which he had slumped, he went and closed the door. "I cannot have Éric hearing all this," he explained. "I have had to close the bar and restaurant. People have been saying things. None of it is true, but they do not want me here." He paused. "I shall stay, though," he added with a steely stare.

"Can you tell me what?"

"They say I only have Éric here so I can have his money. It is so unfair. *Merde*! Sorry! What a mess."

"Who is saying these things?" she asked, although she could guess.

"Monsieur Demille, of course, and some of the other gossips. They spoke to le Maire and I had a warning letter from the *mairie*. Customers have stopped coming in sufficient numbers, and all because of malicious lies."

"This is crazy. Surely there is something we can do," Suzy said.

"If I deny it, people will just think I am protesting too much and if I say nothing people will think it is all true. I cannot win. You must not get involved, Suzy. You have a business to guard now and you cannot afford to get on the wrong side of these small-minded people. I am happy that we can continue to be friends."

Suzy finally got a text from Jo to say she had just pulled into Harriet's driveway. She replied that she would see them both the next day.

The following morning, she trudged down the village and along the little lane by the river. On her way she passed one of the enormous willow trees with its branches sweeping the water. The river was bouncing and gurgling at quite a rate, despite the recent sunny spell. There had been so much rain before that it must still have been seeping through the rocks of the hills all around. Today it was still cracking hot even at this early hour.

Suzy knocked on Harriet's door, and the upper middle section opened to reveal Jo's face through the fancy wrought ironwork covering it.

"I love these French front doors," she said, grinning. "They are so practical and secure. Come on in. I'm going to leave this open to let some air in."

Suzy heard the bolt unfastening and the whole door swung wide. Jo enveloped her in a hug. "Welcome to my new home."

Harriet appeared too and kissed Suzy on both cheeks. Jo and Suzy sat at the living room table while Harriet made tea.

"Nothing like a cup of tea. There're loads of things I love about this place and the people," Jo said, winking at Harriet conspiratorially, "but the French just do not know how to make a good cup of tea. The hot water just isn't hot enough, and the teabags they use are so weak."

"Just don't let anyone hear you criticise anything. Madame Marie has given me the heads up that Monsieur Demille is grumbling at the moment about us English all being licentious!" Suzy warned.

"Is that still going on after the fun we had on the fourteenth of July?" Jo asked.

"I believe so, yes," Suzy answered.

"Monsieur Demille is an old grump," Harriet voiced. "You get them in every village all over the world. He probably secretly wishes he'd had the courage to join in. I met a lot of resistance when I first came to live here with Valentine, but when he realised we were not going to embarrass him, he quietened down."

"You met her when you did that arts course in Arras, didn't you?" Jo asked.

"Yes, and when we realised she was so ill she sold her house to me. French succession laws are very complicated. It meant I could continue living here after she died."

Clearly, they were comfortable talking about their previous lives. Suzy hoped it would work out for Harriet and Jo.

Only a couple of days later, Madame Marie was talking about leaving. Suzy had contacted the estate agent about her own house, and he was conducting a second viewing to the man and his pregnant wife. He thought they would put in a serious offer to buy it. Suzy could not believe this might be true after so short a time.

"I hope it all goes well. As soon as it's sold, I can settle with Madame Marie and get in touch with the notaries in the town near here to see the sale through. It doesn't prevent Madame Marie and her sister, Camille, from leaving, though," Suzy said to Jo at the first opportunity.

"Have you managed to come to an amicable agreement with regard to rent and profits and so on?"

"Yes. We've had to come to a new agreement since she won't be here at all. I'll pay some rent and keep the business going. We've agreed what profits I must give her until we complete the sale, but it's not much. It's all been very friendly."

"It's all formalised properly, is it? You don't want to find she's fleecing you unexpectedly," Jo said.

"She insisted we did it all legally. I'm so excited to be about to take this next leap."

"So, I can at last say I told you so, can I?"

"Yes. I also have this hugely handsome, funny and honest man in my life. I am profoundly grateful."

Suzy was prompted to think some more. *When I'm on my own here, where will I live?* she wondered. *I'm not sure whether I shall stay here or move in with Jean Chri. I don't wish to get in trouble with the village, but nor do I want us to live apart for long.*

The day of Madame Marie's departure finally arrived. She had asked one of the farmers in a nearby village to transport her things. In the end, she had taken her own bedroom furniture but had left the rest.

Before Madame moved out, there was one question to which Suzy had to know the answer. Managing to catch her on her own, she asked with trepidation, "Did you ever come to a more amicable agreement with Jerome? It really was not his fault that he was here that day when I was away, and I feel such a responsibility for your argument."

"No, I have not seen him from that day to this. Some people will crouch in their fortress of vindictive words. I have been guilty of that, I fear. I still do not like the man, but I was wrong to shout so. I should make myself be polite, at least. You have no guilt in that. You thought to help, I know," she said and patted Suzy's hand.

Later, it was with sadness that they hugged and kissed each other farewell. "I owe you so much," Suzy said.

"My dear child, you have been a joy to have with me in my last few months living here, and such a help," Madame Marie said practically. Was that a tear Suzy saw in her eye?

Then she was gone, and Suzy was on her own in the peaceful house. She wandered from room to room with quiet joy. She smelt the furniture polish and fresh flowers; she ran her fingers along the warm, dark wood; the tiles were cool under her feet.

All was silent. There were no crowds outside, no cars and no lorries pounding the street, no rushing through a working lunch and no running to the next meeting. No longer did she have to pretend to be a good hard-working daughter looking after someone else and wishing for nothing more. No longer need she pretend to be a compliant and loving companion with no real zest for living. At last, she had found herself.

She crept into Madame Marie's room. Opening the door furtively, she peered round.

It feels as if I am trespassing, she thought.

There were lighter patches on the wall where pictures and furniture had rested for years and years, but all was clean. There was just a faint lavender smell of the old lady. When the sale was complete, she would need to decorate the room for guests.

Already her mind was buzzing with possibilities for colour schemes and style. As in most French houses, the windows opened inwards and as she stood in the middle of the empty room, with sunshine streaming in, unexpectedly she thought, *This could be an ideal space in which to paint again. Instead of having guests in here, I could use it as my own special studio.*

She was in high spirits again after her moment of calm.

CHAPTER 19

Knowing that Jean Chri was out in a field, Suzy looked out of the window, across to his house. She could see all was quiet there. She understood most of the grain harvest was in, but it wouldn't be long before he had to start on the maize and then when the sunflower heads were heavy with their seeds, it would be their turn.

"I don't grow much beet nowadays," he had told her. "There's a declining market. The local factory closed a couple of years ago, and the next nearest is too far to take a tractor and trailer. I have to hire a wagon to deliver the crop, and that just eats into the profit too much."

"There's an awful lot more to farming than just sowing and gathering," Suzy had said. "You've got to be a scientist and an accountant and all sorts."

"This year we have a small co-operative and have organised the pick-up that way so I'm hoping it is profitable enough. Sugar from beet has been popular in France and beyond since 1811," Jean Chri told Suzy. "You British blockaded the supply routes from the Caribbean," he had teased and laughed. "Good old Napoleon was presented with two sugar loaves from beet and he had factories galore built to manufacture it. I love that you're so interested in my work," he'd said, before he kissed her long and hard yet again

Suzy smiled as she reflected, and then saw his tractor returning. Sudden fear cast a shadow over her happiness. *We must be careful. People will begin to guess that we are having this affair. Please, God, I hope his divorce comes through soon.*

Then she saw him leap down from the tractor and come striding up the road. She felt her excitement rise and could not resist running to the door. She held it open as he climbed the steps. Barely waiting until he was inside, he took her in his arms and with his strong brown hands he stroked her hair, then kissed her as though they hadn't seen each other in forever.

As they pulled apart, he indicated his clothing and he said, "This is the unattractive side of being with a farmer."

As Suzy took the time to give him a proper look, she could see he was filthy.

"My mucky socks are not so romantic when I come in from work. Perhaps you will not love me then!" He gave a deep-throated laugh and she moved forward to kiss him again, regardless of the grubbiness.

"Have a shower and then we could have a glass of wine," she suggested.

"I'll have to sit in just a towel," he said suggestively, raising his eyebrows and tilting his head. "I have no clothes here."

"That expression is why I thought you so arrogant," she said.

"I know. It was a façade."

She put her hand to the side of his face. "No clothes? I'll manage," she said, and she did.

The couple with the dog who came to stay at the B&B were full of funny stories about the holiday they had been having. They said there were bells that rung twice on the hour and every hour through the night; mock bullfights where the husband was the volunteer bull; guesthouse owners who were overenthusiastic about DIY and more. It made Suzy wonder what they would go home and say about her. The dog was well-behaved, although it did not stay in the kennel long. It ended up in their bedroom because of the pitiful noise it made upon being left alone. Fortunately, there was no trace that it had been there once they had left.

There were to be no more guests that weekend, and Suzy had been invited by Jean Chri to have Sunday lunch with Pascal, Amélie and Melodie. She was really looking forward to meeting his family again, but she was also nervous to be taking the place of Jean Chri's soon-to-be ex-wife.

Jean Chri knocked on Suzy's door, and together they walked to his brother's house. It was on the lane next to the river, but further along than Harriet's house. The walk took them twenty minutes, and they were hot and thirsty by the time they arrived. The house was in a little hollow and was absolutely beautiful. Unusually for France, the front garden was a riot of colour with lilies, cornflowers, hydrangea, fuchsias and wild geraniums.

Suzy found her nerves increasing. Jean Chri must have sensed this because he took her hand, squeezed it encouragingly and kissed her cheek, saying, "All will be fine, don't worry, *ma* Suzette." She loved that he knew how she felt without her having to say.

They knocked on the wooden door and it opened almost immediately. Amélie was there, smiling. Pascal came through too and together they greeted Suzy and Jean Chri with kisses and handshakes.

"It is very good to see you again, Suzy." Amélie was warm and enthusiastic, and Suzy knew that all would be alright. Just then, Melodie came bounding in and greeted them both so naturally with her kisses. She immediately went to Jean Chri but then took Suzy's hand to draw her into a cosy little sitting room, where there was a sofa and an old rocking chair with a colourful cushion.

"I am making some socks for Choupinette," Melodie said, holding up her scruffy toy dog which had clearly been loved a lot. "It's her birthday soon. Shh!" She clasped the soft ears with both hands. "Don't tell her, it's a surprise."

Suzy was so happy to play this game and admire the naïve pattern and messy stitching. The rest of the family joined them, and they all approved the little garments in the making.

"Time to put it away now, *ma chérie*," Amélie said. "It is nearly time for dinner. You need to go and wash your hands."

Then she turned to Suzy and said, "Come, Suzy, we shall have *un apéro* before dinner."

Suzy followed her out, through the living room with the large family table and television in the corner and onto the terrace. Amélie indicated a chair.

Before the men joined them, she whispered, "We are so pleased that you and Jean Chri have become friends. You are good for him, I think. He is so much happier and more relaxed now. He was always a little tense before and trying too hard to please other people. Now he is smiling all the time." She did not mention Maryl or her departure, but it seemed to be clear that she was not sorry that she had left.

Shortly, they had a delicious meal and the wine flowed easily, which made for a happy and comfortable atmosphere. When they had eventually finished eating, Melodie retrieved her sewing and dragged her chair as close to Suzy as it would go.

"Melodie," her mum remonstrated, "Suzy does not want to do that now."

"Absolutely, I do," Suzy reassured her. "Choupinette needs her present finishing, doesn't she, Melodie?"

As the afternoon drew on, Suzy felt more and more a part of this family. Jean Chri was attentive and ensured that she was involved in the conversations. From time to time, he touched her arm or her shoulder or rested a hand on her leg. She relished this reassuring attention. His broad smile encompassed all around him and she reflected upon what Amélie had said earlier, with a warm pleasure inside.

"It is so hot that it is difficult to move much," Amélie observed.

They were all happy to be lazy. After a while Melodie crept onto Suzy's knee and fell asleep. Her hair was damp, and her little body was hot against her, but she didn't mind.

"I think there is rain in the air," Jean Chri observed. "The clouds are building. Look over there."

"I can hardly believe it after such a dry spell. It has been a year of bizarre weather," Pascal said.

"Yes, we had all that rain and now this heat," Amélie added. "I almost wish it would rain again just to refresh the atmosphere."

"I could do with some rain for the beet now the grain harvest is in," Jean Chri said, "but I hope no more of the soil gets washed away as it did before."

"You all sound like the English, discussing the weather." Suzy laughed and they joined in.

As the clouds piled up, the breeze increased. Jean Chri scooped up Melodie from Suzy's knee, carried her indoors and placed her on a cushion. As they cleared the table, she stirred and awoke. She was hot and thirsty, and started to grizzle.

"Come with me, little one," Jean Chri said as he scooped her up again. "Let's find you a drink."

He took her into the kitchen, where Amélie was making coffee. As Pascal brought in the cloth from the table outside, they returned. Jean Chri had been teasing Melodie, and her grumpiness was forgotten. She smiled up at him and Suzy as she yawned, stretched and rubbed her ear. Reaching for Choupinette, she was happy again already.

"Can I stay at Suzy's and Uncle's and Aunt Maryl's house?" she asked Pascal as he came in through the French doors.

The adults looked at each other and Suzy did't know what to say.

"She hasn't seen her aunt for quite a while, but she has never said anything before," Pascal said. "To be honest, we have put off this moment."

"Aunt Maryl is not here anymore," Jean Chri said gently.

"Why not?" asked Melodie.

"She wanted to go and live somewhere else, with some other people."

Melodie shrugged. "Well, can I stay with Suzy and Uncle Jean Chri, then?"

The question presented Suzy and Jean Chri with a new dilemma. Neither of them had stayed with each other overnight before, since they were so wary of gossip.

Amélie sent Melodie into the kitchen to fetch the sugar. Suzy soon realised this was a ploy to get her out of earshot.

"If you are both happy with it, I am sure we are." Amélie glanced at Pascal with eyebrows raised in a question.

"Absolutely," he responded. "She loves to stay with you, little brother, and if Suzy is there too, so much the better."

With a pink face, Suzy glanced at Jean Chri. He winked. Her tummy swooped and she smiled her response.

At that point, Melodie trotted back into the room, very carefully guarding the pot of sugar lumps for the coffee. They sat around the table, waiting for her to put the pot safely on the table. Silently signalling across at Amélie for approval, Suzy asked Melodie if she would like to stay.

"Oh, yes please." She hopped from one foot to the other and clapped her hands. Her blonde hair bounced and her face radiated pleasure. "I shall go and get my nightie and toothbrush. Choupinette can come too, can't she?"

"I hope she will," Jean Chri agreed. "It wouldn't be such fun without her, would it?"

As she left the room, there sounded a distant rumble.

"Was that thunder?" asked Jean Chri. "Will Melodie be frightened if there is a storm? Maybe you would prefer her to stay here."

"She'll be fine. She will sleep right through it, and if it arrives before she goes to bed, she will not be scared. She thought the last one we had was very exciting," Amélie replied.

It was not long before it was time for them to collect up Melodie and all her paraphernalia and head for home.

"I'll drive you," Pascal said. "I know it is not far, but Melodie's overnight bag has ended up with quite a few extra bits in it and she is starting to get tired again."

They arrived at Jean Chri's house. Thanks had already been said, and so Suzy hurried indoors with Melodie's bag. She was very conscious of being seen by the other villagers.

Pascal said to Melodie, "I'll see you tomorrow, little one." He smiled at Jean Chri. "I hope you all get a good night."

There was another distant rumble and they hurried indoors before there were any large splatters of rain. There was an unnatural greenish tinge around the dark clouds that had finally blocked out the sun.

CHAPTER 20

Jean Chri and Melodie hurried indoors to join Suzy. The sky was dark, although it was not late.

As Amélie had suggested, Melodie was completely unperturbed by the change in the weather. She happily skipped from room to room, ensuring all was as she remembered from her previous visit.

Jean Chri took Suzy's hand and drew her to him, for which she was grateful. It did seem very strange and she felt like a usurper. When she had been there previously, they'd been carried away on a wave of passion. This time, Suzy was aware that they were making an even greater commitment to a long-term future. Still no such words had passed between them on the subject, but she was sure they both were certain of their advancing relationship.

Melodie reappeared clutching Choupinette and asked, "Can I have something to eat, please?"

"Of course, *ma petite chérie*. But have you really got space? It's not long since you had a big dinner," Jean Chri said.

"Mmm, I'm really hungry," Melodie answered.

Jean Chri sorted out something for her, glancing at Suzy from time to time to ensure she was alright. Suzy smiled at him as she watched. This felt so right.

Before sitting at the table, Melodie came and took Suzy's hand, pulling her to the seat next to hers. She felt a rush of warmth for this beautiful child. It was almost an ache, and a feeling that she had not experienced before. It surprised her.

There was a distant rumble of thunder, and suddenly the bushes outside the window swayed in the stiff breeze.

"We are definitely in for a storm. It's coming closer," Suzy remarked. "Perhaps it will clear the air."

Getting up to look out of the window, she saw the wind was now whipping the trees, showing the paler undersides of the leaves and whirling clouds of dust. Large splatters of rain hit the window. Suzy felt a flitter of nervous excitement as she saw a flash of lightning in the distance. Glancing across at Melodie, she saw that she had not even noticed the approaching weather; Jean Chri was teasing her and she was giggling.

There was another clap of thunder and then another.

"There must be more than one storm approaching. The gap between the lightning and the noise is getting shorter," Jean Chri said to Suzy.

The rain that had been threatening for so long was now coming down in slanting rods.

As Melodie finished her last mouthful, she joined Suzy and her uncle. Jean Chri lifted her up to see out of the window, enclosing her in their circle.

"Well, little one, what would you like to do now? Shall we play a card game? *Jeu des Sept Familles*, perhaps?"

"In England we call it Happy Families." Suzy smiled up at Jean Chri.

They settled comfortably at the table with their cards as the storm approached and the thunder rumbled more frequently. Then there was an almighty crash, indicating it was very close indeed. Melodie laughed at how they all jumped with surprise.

"Oh, that was funny," she said. "You nearly dropped your cards, Suzy."

As they played, the storm rumbled further away but it continued to rain hard. There were distant sheets of lightning that registered in Suzy's peripheral vision as the thunder gradually receded. Eventually they finished their game and it was time for Melodie to go to bed.

"Will you take me, Suzy?"

They stood and Melodie took her hand again as they walked along the hallway to her room. Jean Chri and Maryl had decorated it for her some time ago. It was pretty and delicate, and the bed had a little pink canopy of voile coming from a tiara-shaped circlet hanging from the ceiling. The bedding did not match, however, and looked as if it had been borrowed from elsewhere. Suzy was determined to change this as soon as possible. She was conscious that she needed to make her mark in this house, but it seemed insensitive to sweep in and change things too much, too quickly.

Melodie took a thin, colourful book from the shelf once she was washed and her teeth were brushed. She asked Suzy to read to her once she was tucked up. Suzy lay on top of the bed next to her. It was a simple book, the language of which Suzy could understand easily now, and she read with meaning in her voice. Then she kissed Melodie goodnight as the little girl snuggled down.

As she headed back to the living room and Jean Chri, the ringing of Suzy's mobile phone was nearly drowned out by the noise of the rain hitting the windows and the roof. It was Jo. "I wondered how your afternoon went?"

"It was good. In fact, better than that. They made me so welcome and now we have Melodie staying with us for the night. She really wanted to come and Amélie was actually encouraging us to be together tonight."

Jo started to say, "Wow, that's…" A tremendous crash of thunder sounded close. Suzy heard Harriet speak to Jo. "This rain sounds so heavy, I might just check the cellar."

"It should be fine, shouldn't it?" Jo asked blithely. "Do it if you want to, of course."

Jo carried on talking to Suzy, who could hear what was going on in the background. Harriet crossed the room and opened the little door. Suzy pictured her ducking her head and going down the first two steps. "The pump has come on, but it's not very deep," Suzy heard. "That last clap of thunder was close by. I hope nothing was hit. There has been a lot of sheet lightning, but I did see some that was forked too. Anyway, it seems to be moving away now."

"Is Harriet worried about the storm?" Suzy asked with concern.

"I really don't like it," Harriet answered. Jo had put it onto speakerphone. "A house across the road was once struck by lightning. It went through the roof and broke the toilet in half."

"Lucky no-one was sitting on it at the time," Jo said and Suzy imagined her smiling.

"It did blow all the sockets out of the walls, apparently. I think ever since then, I've been a little nervous."

"We are low down here. It would hit something else before us. We'll be alright, I'll make sure of that," Jo said confidently.

"I am so lucky to have found you," Harriet said with feeling.

"It's getting dark very early tonight," Suzy said. "Can you see the river?"

"Not really. The path dips down to our house so we're slightly below the bank and the water here."

"I'm sure the level in the cellar is rising," she heard Harriet's voice again from a distance.

"Surely the pump will deal with that won't it?" Suzy asked Jo. "Harriet gets it serviced, doesn't she?"

"I do, annually." Harriet must have returned from the cellar.

"No need to worry, I'm sure," Jo said. "I need to get an early night. We had an impromptu games evening here yesterday, with a couple from another village. All the wine and funning around has left me exhausted today. We played everything from tiddlywinks to outdoor quoits."

"That sounds fun, and if I know you," Suzy said, "it was a late one."

Jo laughed. "Well … more early morning. We invented several games with made-up rules and called it garden Olympics. It did all become a little ludicrous the more wine we had, I do admit."

"I'm off to bed. Night Suzy," Harriet called.

Jo gave a loud yawn. "I'm climbing the stairs as we speak. See you soon."

Jean Chri had laid out two glasses and found an open bottle of wine by the time Suzy returned to the living room.

"This will relax you," he said, understanding her tension. "We'll have a quiet supper and an early night, shall we?"

This suited her well, and they ate a simple light meal since they had eaten so heartily with Pascal and Amélie earlier.

Only a little later, holding hands as best they could in the narrow space along the hallway to Jean Chri's room, they peeped in on Melodie. They saw she had pushed the covers off and had her arms flung above her head. Jean Chri let go of Suzy and gently tucked the covers back in, stroking the hair from her face and softly planting a kiss on the top of her head. She stirred but did not wake.

Pushing their door closed, Jean Chri turned to Suzy. His brown arms encircled her, and she rested her head against his chest with a sigh, fitting in that crook of his shoulder perfectly with her right hand against his heart.

Slowly he released her and gently took her cardigan and slid it down her arms. He kissed her neck behind her ear, causing her to shiver with pleasure. Next, he slowly undid the buttons at the front of her shirt. As he finished undressing her and she was finally naked, he shed his shirt and trousers quickly.

By unspoken agreement, they lay together and drifted into sleep without further intimacy. Suzy was completely content.

Later, while it was still dark, Suzy felt his hands on her body; those strong, brown hands that she loved so much. With the rain still lashing the windows, they made love slowly. She relished the fact that he tried to please her and considered her first.

Afterwards, they drifted back to sleep in a haze of love and satisfaction.

The next morning was unnaturally dim as Suzy, wrapped in a raincoat and wearing wellingtons, hurried down the road to the restaurant for some milk and eggs. Jerome was making a half-hearted attempt to tidy his kitchen a little.

"Éric, I need you to go and collect all the eggs, as many as you can find," Jerome said calmly.

"What, now?" Éric asked.

"Yes, now, as many as you can. Look in all the usual places and any others you can think of. I need as many as possible."

"But it's pouring with rain. The light is not good. Can't I do it tomorrow?"

"Never mind on my account," Suzy said, as Jerome placed a coffee in front of her.

"No, I need them now," Jerome said clearly.

Éric put on his raincoat with a sigh and closed the door behind him, shrugging his hood up and hunching against the weather. Jerome stood at the window long enough to watch him cross the courtyard in the unusually leaden light, heading for the barn.

"I'll be back in a minute," he said. "I've got supplies down here," he called over his shoulder as he went down to the cellar, where he had been storing jars of vegetables and fruit from the garden. Suzy knew he had spent many hours preparing and preserving his home-grown produce, as he did each year. He and Éric would have had eaten quite a bit over the weeks. "There's still a lot down here," came his distant call. "There's some wooden boxes in a dark corner down here. I'm just packing the preserving jars."

He staggered back up the steps with a heavy looking box. "I'm not sure why but I think we must do this. Sometimes I know these things."

Suzy wondered if his simple country life had given him a sixth sense about these things.

"Can I help?" Suzy asked.

"No, no. You take your coffee."

After he had filled several boxes, Jerome began the heavy work of carrying them upstairs to the living room. He was still trying to complete this task when Éric returned with a bucket that was full of eggs. There were duck eggs with waxy, thick shells; bantam eggs that were small, but which would have a large yolk inside; chicken eggs that were both brown and varied shades of cream, since Jerome kept any number of different varieties of hens.

"It's truly awful out there," Éric said as a crack of thunder almost overhead caused them all to stoop involuntarily. "Why are you collecting all that up here?" He suddenly noticed all the food that had appeared from the cellar.

"I just thought," Jerome answered, "that we have such a lot and perhaps we could give some to Suzy. She is very kind to us."

She understood he hoped the fib would be enough to keep Éric happy, and when he shrugged, she gathered he could hardly explain to himself, never mind Éric, why he needed to do this. Éric did not pursue the matter. He took off his coat and went to hang it somewhere to drip dry.

As the thunder receded, Jerome shrugged his shoulders at Suzy and said, "I have chickens and rabbits in the barn. Maybe I'll leave them for the time being. Perhaps I'm being overcautious and none of this is necessary. I just have this feeling of impending doom."

"I certainly hope not," Suzy said and smiled at him nervously.

While the various households were busy, the rain continued to pelt down. That afternoon, Pierre le Bec, the mayor, knocked on Jean Chri's door. "The automatic mechanism of the weir downstream has operated and opened slightly to allow more water through. but it's not functioning as it should because reeds and grass have built up during the previous few months had not been cleared efficiently by Marc."

"Come in, come in," Jean Chri said and Pierre stood dripping on the stone-flagged floor.

"I only just asked him, yet again, to do this at the end of last week. He responded in his usual way, and the job is yet to be done. Monsieur Demille was aware of this and was straight on the telephone to me."

"What did he have to say?"

"'It really is not good enough,' he said. You know how he is. 'I'm sure the river level is up, and the weir cannot be efficient as it should be if Marc does not do his work properly.' Oh la, he did go on." *Monsieur le Maire* sighed audibly. "I have set him targets and if he still does not comply and achieve them, he will be sacked. I assured Monsieur Demille of that."

Jean Chri nodded but said nothing, understanding that Pierre needed to get all this out.

"Monsieur Demille has demanded that at the next meeting of *le conseil*, he wants it brought up for discussion. 'There is a group of us who are thinking this,' he told me. 'Who else would like this brought up?' I asked him. 'Oh, I couldn't possibly say over the telephone,' he said, of course, 'but I can assure you that everyone thinks the same as I. It is only me who has the courage to speak out about it.' Honestly!"

"Right. I understand exactly," Jean Chri said. "In the meantime, I need to go out myself, right now, and check on the state of the weir. Are you able to join me to help?"

"Wait while I get my coat and boots." He turned to Suzy. "I think Melodie better stay another night. It's raining so hard. I'll ring my brother."

Putting on his raincoat, hat and wellington boots, Jean Chri trudged through the gloomy evening down the lane to the end of the village with *Monsieur le Maire*. The rain dripped down his neck and he was soon soaked. As they suspected, there was a build-up of debris, but they were convinced, correctly, that it was not an emergency under the present circumstances.

CHAPTER 21

All night and the following morning the rain continued. It was steady and heavy. Not long after dawn as the light improved, Pierre le Bec called on Marc the *bricoleur*, the handyman, and Jean Chri, to accompany him in clearing the debris from the weir. They all trudged down together.

"The river water level is up a bit but not too much, as far as I can see," observed Pierre, as he looked down between the trees to the river.

He received a grunt from Marc, which caused the perennial roll-up to bob up and down from his bottom lip. "I was going to do this as soon as the weather clears up," he said.

Pierre ignored this, knowing it was extremely unlikely that he would have got around to it, and looked across at Jean Chri who grinned behind Marc's back. Together they plodded down the steep slope, heading for the lane and downstream to the weir.

"There is a lot of mud coming down this slope," Pierre said, with a frown. "It may cause the same problem as before. I hope not. The drains are so old they are not up to this."

As they reached the bottom, their fears were realised. Water was starting to run across the road.

"Will you come and sweep the mud away with your tractor and rig like you did last time? Let's get on and see to this rubbish blocking the weir, first."

Again, the mayor was treated to a grunt of reluctant agreement from Marc.

Pierre le Bec, Jean Chri, and *le bricoleur* struggled to put on their waders in the pouring rain. Eventually, they tentatively entered the water. It was quite deep, but they man-handled their bill hooks as with years of experience.

Gradually they grabbed heavy wreaths of long bullrushes and dead roots that had flowed with the current over quite a long period of time. The mud on the bottom was cloying at their feet and made the task more difficult. It was a slow business. Eventually there were enough weeds removed and suddenly, the water poured through the weir. They had to balance against the drag and pull of it. The level dropped suddenly. They continued to work, and it was at least an hour later when *Monsieur le Maire* deemed they had done enough.

"Wake up, wake up, *mon oncle*. It's time for breakfast. Suzy, it's time to get up now," Melodie chirped. "Choupinette is very, very hungry."

"Urgh! What time is it?"

Jean Chri flung his arms above his head and grinned sideways at Suzy. "Early," he said. "Very early. I'm used to it, though. This, too, is the life of a farmer."

She smiled back at him. "Mmm," she murmured. "It's only just light. What's the time?" She rolled sideways. "Fetch me a big bath towel, little one." Melodie found a towel, threw it at Suzy and danced off. As she went, Suzy called, "Get the bowls out ready for the hot chocolate."

Swinging her legs round, she rose from the warm bed and wrapped the towel around herself. She turned to Jean Chri at the door. "It doesn't often rain for this long in one go, does it?"

"No, it does not." Jean Chri rose. "I better take a look down in the village and see what the situation is."

"You shower first if you want. I'll grab one after I've got Melodie her breakfast," said Suzy.

As Melodie and Suzy busied themselves in the kitchen, Suzy was sure she heard a very strange ripping sound. As Jean Chri entered the room, she said, "What on earth was that noise?"

"I heard nothing over the shower," he replied.

Moving to the window, Suzy looked out, but through the heavy rain and wind she could see little. "It really is grim out there," she said.

Jean Chri took a piece of bread and butter, gulped down some hot chocolate and, reaching for his coat, he was just heading for the door when the telephone rang. He and Suzy looked at each other, wondering who could be ringing this early.

"That can't be a good sign," he whispered as he moved towards the phone. He answered the call. "It is *Monsieur le Maire*," he said to Suzy.

She watched his face and saw an exasperated look flit across his features. Then he nodded.

"I'll go straight away," he said and rang off. "That was Pierre telling me the soil is being washed down from the fields yet again. I shall have to go and get the tractor out and do what I can to sweep it away from the drain covers. It sets like concrete."

"It's still raining so hard. Won't it just keep coming down the hill?"

"*Bah oui!*" Jean Chri shrugged. "It seems any action will not be effective." Reaching again for his coat, he headed for the door. "Will you phone Pascal and Amélie at a more sociable hour and say we are happy to keep Melodie until a bit later, when the rain should have stopped, unless they want to come and collect her?"

He gave Suzy a hurried kiss as he disappeared through the door.

Jerome and Éric were trundling an old wheelbarrow full of boxes filled with jars. It was hard going as the water was now nearly knee-deep across the road. They waved to Jean Chri, who was trying to sweep some of the mud and water away with little success.

"Where are you off to with all that?" Jean Chri called to them.

Upon hearing Jerome's reply, he responded, "She's at my house with Melodie, but I'm about to ring her and tell her to take the little one up to hers. Leave that at the top of the steps there and I'll take it in for her when I have finished here."

They saluted an understanding.

Having deposited the goods, Jean Chri saw the pair as they approached his own house and saw a light come on. Jerome was encouraged that Suzy was up and about. He left Éric at the gate and approached the front door again, knocking with determination.

Suzy finally answered. "Jerome," she exclaimed. "It's very early. Is everything alright?"

"I've brought you some eggs and preserved vegetables and fruit; things that might come in handy. I've left them by your door," he answered sheepishly.

"Oh, thank you. Well, please do come in. Jean Chri has gone to see if he can help sweep the mud and water from the road."

"We saw him," Jerome responded.

Suzy offered him a coffee, which he accepted gratefully and beckoned for Éric to come. Melodie politely kissed him good morning, but Suzy saw her surreptitiously rub her face.

"You are prickly," she said honestly to Jerome.

"Sorry. I came out quickly this morning. All this rain is worrying."

"Do you think you should go and get dressed now?" Suzy prompted Melodie. She was rightly concerned that Jerome would say something that might upset the little girl. Melodie skipped to her room.

"The hillsides are so steep, and the valley floor is not wide. It is raining too hard. If the riverbank gives way, many will have a problem," Jerome continued.

"Surely it has rained hard like this before," Suzy argued gently.

"Yes, yes, of course. I am just being a silly old man."

"Is this why you have brought me all that food? In case there is a problem?"

"Well, maybe." He looked awkward.

"Jerome, you are the kindest person," Suzy reassured him.

It was not long after this, as they finished their coffee, that Suzy's phone rang.

"Hello? Oh Jo, hello. You're phoning early. Are you okay?"

"Is Jean Chri there? We've got a major problem here."

"What is it?" Suzy asked with concern.

"We jumped awake this morning. Did you hear that roaring, ripping sound?"

"I certainly heard something."

"It sounded like it was right outside our house. Anyway…"
Harriet joined in.

"It sounded like a roaring, splitting, hissing, splashing sound," Harriet said as she struggled to describe the racket she had heard.

"I told her to calm down," said Jo. "I hadn't heard anything at all. I was sound asleep."

"Jo, tell me. What's the problem?" Suzy demanded.

"Harriet opened the shutter. Nearly blinded me."

"Jo! Get on with it. What's up?"

"A paperback book is floating past the third step."

"Hell's bells. Look at that," Harriet said now. "What do we do? We've got murky water filling our living room. It's covering the garden. It's clearly spilled from the riverbank."

The sound of Harriet opening the window to lean out came down the phone and her voice called from a distance, "There's a large willow tree lying across the river, making an effective dam. Half the bank where it once stood has been washed away. It's still pouring with rain." She shut the window again.

"We must get dressed quickly," Jo said. "I rang *Monsieur le Maire* but there was no reply. Jean Chri will help us, won't he?"

The situation sounded serious but Suzy told her that Jean Chri was out in his tractor, clearing the water from the road. She told her friend that she would phone him straight away, and she did just that.

"I'll drive the tractor up there now," Jean Chri responded to Suzy's urgent call. "If they are in trouble, others will be too. Take Melodie and get up to your house now. If the tree that Jo told you about moves, and all that water is freed, it will rush down the village and the drains are already swamped."

"Don't worry about us. We're fine, but we will go," Suzy reassured him. She did not say more, since he was clearly so preoccupied.

Jean Chri phoned the mobile of Pierre le Bec. He quickly explained and told him to ask for help from another farmer to rescue any others who may be in danger.

"We've just cleared the weir again and the water level suddenly dropped. I hope we haven't caused the banks to collapse," Pierre said in a worried voice. He said he would phone *les pompiers*. Their ladders and pumps would be useful.

Jean Chri drove as carefully as he could along what used to be the lane. It was daunting, because there were so few landmarks to judge where the lane ended and the river began. He felt himself sweating around his neck, and his heart was thumping. His tractor wheels were massive, but that would not help him if he steered too close to the bank.

He passed another tree, now prone across the river with its massive roots half in and half out of the water. There was no sign of the bank, and he guessed there was a large gouge out of it. Eventually he arrived at what he judged was Harriet's driveway. He could see only one of the gateposts sticking up out of the water. Jo and Harriet were at the window and opened it as he arrived. Harriet was crying.

"Are you both alright?"

They nodded and Jo shouted back, "What shall we do?"

"If I raise the bucket really close, can you climb out into it?"

"Bloody Nora," he heard Harriet say. "I don't know if I can do that."

"Well, it's that or stay here on your own," Jo said.

"Can you come along to the window at this end?" Jean Chri called up.

"Yes. It's a date. Hang on and we'll see you there. Make mine a large glass of red," Jo joked.

By the time they reappeared at the nearest window, Jean Chri had lifted the bucket as close to them as he possibly could. They opened the window and even Jo grimaced as they both saw what they needed to do.

"It really will be safe and steady," he tried to reassure them.

"I'll go first," Jo said to Harriet. "Then I'll be able to help you."

"Okay," Harriet replied in a wobbly voice as she dashed her sleeve across her face to soak up the tears.

"Shite, shite, shite," Jo whispered to herself. She hoisted first one leg over the sill and then, squatting astride the opening, she swung the other long leg over and round so that she was sitting facing the outside. "I'll be brave," she said, glancing over her shoulder to where Harriet waited. She launched herself carefully forward into the bucket. It wavered a little, but she had to admit that she felt safer than she thought she would. Turning back to the window and to Harriet, she stretched out her hand and gave an encouraging nod and a smile. "Come on, it's easier than you think. I will keep you safe, you know I will. You are precious to me," she added quietly, for Harriet's ears alone.

With that encouragement, Harriet followed Jo's example and carefully swung her legs over and round, lowering herself gradually into the bucket next to Jo.

With them both safely rescued, Jean Chri turned his thoughts to the subsequent tricky move. He was nowhere near as confident as he had sounded. He had to manoeuvre the tractor backwards and round into the lane until he was facing the right way for the return journey.

Finally reaching the road into the village, Jean Chri mentally heaved a sigh of relief. Reaching drier land, he lowered the bucket scoop and the two women climbed out unsteadily. The weirdness of the situation finally brought a smile to Harriet's face.

"Go up to Suzy's house. You will be safe there," he shouted down from his cab.

As he prepared to turn around and head back to see if anyone else was in the same predicament, he saw Suzy at the door of her house. Standing in front of her was Melodie. She blew him a kiss and he appreciated her smiling encouragement.

While Jean Chri was making another similar run to rescue a pair of middle-aged sisters who lived together, Alexandre and Nicolas hailed him from their tractor. They had come out to see what could be done to help.

Jean Chri and the brothers together made three more similar trips. It was significantly more difficult to persuade Monsieur Demille and his wife, Florence, to climb down into the tractor bucket. Jean Chri had to promise to turn his head so that he would not see her big pink knickers. Her husband had to promise her all kinds of things that Jean Chri was pleased he could not hear.

Gradually people were delivered to Suzy's house, since it was well above flood level.

CHAPTER 22

With people arriving at her house in various states of uncertainty, undress and fear, Suzy was kept remarkably busy. Some were chilly and shaking; others were robust and overcompensating for how they were really feeling.

Initially everyone was in a slight state of shock and thus far had not resumed the antagonisms of previous days, even when Jerome's presence became obvious. Suzy had thought he and Éric were headed for their own home, but it was typical of him to come up and help her, having become aware of all the activity in the village and the tractors passing his house with their strange cargo.

Blankets were found for those who were shivering. Florence Demille was busy telling everyone what a dangerous time she'd had — how she had nearly fallen head-first into the water — and bemoaning the fact that her lovely house was ruined. She seemed unaware that others were suffering the same fate.

Jo and Harriet were helping to pass hot drinks around and everyone expressed their gratitude.

Jerome seemed in his element, keeping a permanent flow of coffee on the go and washing up in between other housekeeping activities. He had detailed Éric to light a fire in the log burner, so the older folk could gather round and keep warm.

Suzy had plenty to do, making up beds and ensuring towels were in place. As she rushed between bedrooms, she had a heart-stopping moment when she hoped Jean Chri was alright and not putting himself in too much danger.

Passing through the living room, Suzy took a moment to look out of the window. The rain had eased off quite a lot. She scanned the roads to see if there was any sign of the familiar green tractor, but there wasn't. Perhaps Jean Chri had resumed his mud-cleaning activities.

There was a distant rumble. Was that more thunder? Suzy sighed. Jo and Harriet got up from their seats, and Jo gave Suzy a hug.

"What else can we do to help?"

"If you could help with the beds, that would be marvellous. Let me show you where to find sheets and pillowcases. We'll need to move a mattress from one of the family rooms to another room, as well, to make an extra sleeping space," Suzy said.

Eventually Suzy heard the deep engine of the tractor, and Jean Chri arrived at the door.

"I'm absolutely worn out," he told Suzy. "I'm grimy from head to toe, too."

She placed her arm around him and guided him indoors, giving him a warm and welcoming kiss on his cheek. "You look exhausted."

Alexandre and Nicolas came up the steps just then.

"Come on in," Suzy said at the door. "Come and have a coffee."

"We'll just have a quick one," Jean Chri said, "but then we must go back out. There is still a couple stuck on the other side of the valley, and they need a lift across to their son's house. They're not in danger, but they're naturally upset and worried. There's still no sign of *les pompiers*. Have you been in touch with Pascal or Amélie?"

"I've rung several times, but there is no reply. I've tried Pascal's mobile number and the landline," Suzy responded, encouraging him to sit for five minutes while he drank his coffee. "Perhaps the cables are down," she added, trying to allay the worry etched on Jean Chri's face.

"He should be answering his mobile, though." He continued to look anxious. "Is Melodie alright?"

"She was asking when her mummy or daddy will come. She's in one of the bedrooms at the moment with Jo. She's polishing the furniture. There's probably none left in the tin by now." Suzy smiled at him.

"She loves doing that," her uncle said.

They were so preoccupied that they did not immediately notice the darkening sky, but there was another rumble. Shortly after, there was a flash of lightning and a louder crash of thunder that had Madame Demille squealing and in tears.

Jo returned with Melodie, who ran to Jean Chri as soon as she saw him. He lifted her onto his knee.

"You are very grubby," she said. Then she turned to Suzy. "Madame Demille is very noisy."

Suzy grinned at her and nodded. "She likes a little drama, I think," she said quietly. "She's fine really. She's not brave like you, though. You know it's just the weather, don't you?"

The little girl nodded solemnly.

Harriet looked worried at the sound outside, but Jo placed her hand on her shoulder and gave a comforting squeeze. Harriet responded with a small smile.

"I must go again," Jean Chri stated and rose wearily. The two lads got up too, but Jean Chri waved them down. "No, you two stay here. I shan't be long, and you have done more than enough. Stay for dinner. You can be of help here, I'm sure."

"Please take care, and don't take any risks," Suzy could not help saying, despite her resolve not to fuss.

He kissed and hugged her warmly, disregarding the villagers. He no longer cared about the gossipmongers, and neither did she.

Hunched in his coat with the hood up, Jean Chri headed back to his tractor and wondered what he should do first. He was aware of the old couple across the valley, but he was really worried about his brother and sister-in-law.

There was still no sign of *les pompiers*. They must have been having trouble getting up the valley, or else they were overwhelmed with emergency calls. He decided to ring the mayor to find out if he had any information.

"Is there any news of *les pompiers* arriving soon?" he asked when Pierre answered. "We could do with their ladders and medical expertise."

"There is still no sign at all," Pierre responded.

Jean Chri told of what had been accomplished so far.

"How is Suzy coping?" Pierre asked. "It is very good of her to care for so many people."

"She has very competent help from Jerome. He arrived early this morning with tonnes of food in jars from his cellar that he has been preserving since last year. I don't know how he knew it would be needed."

"Well, perhaps we need to review the village position with him. It has been complicated with rumours flying. He hasn't helped his own situation either. He can be quite volatile, and it doesn't take much to wind up some others. It seems like we owe him a few favours, though."

Finishing the call, Jean Chri rang Pascal again but there was still no answer. He made a decision. He would see if he could reach Pascal's house. It was further along the lane from Harriet's, but he was increasingly concerned. The old couple would just have to wait a short time. He knew they were not in immediate danger, just stranded and a little worried.

As Jean Chri turned his vehicle round, there was a flash of forked lightning and an almighty crash of thunder, which made him jump. Not more rain, surely. His fears were shortly realised, though, as he carefully drove along the road and through the floodwater caused by the blocked drains. The raindrops began again in earnest, firing down like bullets from a nearly black sky. The noise was deafening.

He had gone a couple of hundred metres along the lane, taking great care not to stray too close to where the riverbank used to be, when suddenly, above the noise of the rain on the tractor roof, Jean Chri heard a deep rumbling, rushing noise.

Suzy, in the warmth of her house halfway up the hill, heard the same sound, as did the others who were sharing her safe retreat. Those who were younger rushed to the windows, and the elderly struggled to their feet and limped to look out too. There was little to see from there. The lie of the land and the thick canopy of the trees bordering the roads sheltered the view of the valley floor. They could only see down the road. After a few moments, the others resumed their huddle around the fire and those who were working continued with their tasks, thinking that maybe another tree had come down.

The first clue that something momentously dangerous was occurring was the sight of a huge tree advancing horizontally at a treacherous speed through the water. The river was now so wide, and was a churning, boiling mass of muddied brown foam and froth. It was unrecognisable. Jean Chri knew it was not the old willow tree he had just seen. It had come from higher up the valley.

There was another tree not far behind it being tossed like a splinter even though that one must be twelve or fourteen metres long. Was that the noise that Suzy thought she'd heard early that morning — trees being ripped from the earth? Perhaps they had been stuck somewhere and were now freed.

Impaled and disembowelled upon the side branches of the larger tree was a car that was being flung around in the deep, rushing water. It was a blue Citroën, which was quite old. Jean Chri knew this car. It was his brother's. His heart thumped and he grew breathless. Were Pascal or Amélie inside?

Surely they would not have been stupid enough to try and drive a car in this weather, he thought angrily.

They would have been worried for Melodie, though. Maybe they had set out before the river burst its banks. Clearly trees had been falling and had blocked the river higher up. Had dammed water suddenly given way? If they were in the car, they would have been in it for some time. Jean Chri shuddered.

Why were they not answering the phone? Perhaps it was submerged, and they were safe upstairs in their house. Where was all this water coming from?

Jean Chri was momentarily puzzled. Had the tree swept down earlier? Had it been wedged somewhere? He had no idea.

He was horrified to see the mangled metal swept along like a toy. It was only then that he realised it was the advance warning of a colossal wall of water, three metres high and surging towards him with speed.

Jean Chri understood that the nature of the steep-sided, narrow valley meant that he could not avoid the water pouring into his path. He just had time to open the door of his cab, thinking that he did not want to drown trapped in that tiny space. Then the whole tractor slewed around with the powerful force of the deluge. He clung on.

He felt rather than saw rocks and debris, trees and mud being rolled along as well. His enormous tractor was tipped over.

"Suzy," he called. "I'm so sorry."

And he was hurled forwards in to the murk.

"Melodie," Suzy called, aware that the little girl was worried and lacking attention. "Melodie, will you help me?" Giving her a hug, she thought to keep the little one busy.

"Would you ask the ladies who are sitting by the fire to play Happy Families with you? I really think it would cheer them up, and they would really enjoy your company."

"Will my mummy and daddy be here soon?" Melodie asked with a frown.

"I'm sure they will arrive as soon as they can, *ma minette*," Suzy reassured her.

Looking over her shoulder to make sure the child was alright, she went to find Jerome in the kitchen. Suzy was reassured as she saw Melodie skip across with her pack of cards. The older ladies greeted her with smiles and hugs.

"Jerome, we will need to give all these people dinner soon," Suzy said as she entered the kitchen. "I'm really not sure what to do at such short notice."

Jerome showed her what he had prepared so far. "We don't have much meat for this number of people, but I think we should be fine. I can make it seem like more if I add these." He held up a jar of preserved root vegetables. "We have plenty of eggs and milk, so for dessert I wondered about a simple crème Anglaise. I could make some little biscuits to go with it. It will be plain but satisfying, and people will feel better for having food inside them."

"You are so clever and I am profoundly grateful." She gave him a big hug. "I would be very hard-pressed to manage this without you. We all owe you thanks."

After a few minutes, they all heard a helicopter. It sounded as if it was circling around, quite close. En masse they moved to the windows to see what was occurring. The helicopter was indeed nearby, hanging in the sky but very low indeed. The distinctive red and yellow colours informed them all that this was a medical helicopter. Help was at hand.

It was so close to the ground that the identification number on its tail fin was clearly visible.

"Is it landing?"

"What's going on?"

"It's really close."

"*Que Dieu nous aide,*" Madame Demille whispered, crossing herself and raising her eyes heavenward.

Instead of landing, the medicopter hung just above the trees, causing them to writhe about even more riotously than before.

"He must be an incredibly skilful pilot. Look at the wind driving the rain almost horizontal," one of the men said.

Between the leaves, the watchers now saw a mass of churning water.

"Look, look," someone cried. "He's moving off."

Suzy looked around for Melodie.

"What is happening?" the child asked someone plaintively.

Suzy called her over, lifted her into her arms and spoke to her calmly although her own heart was racing.

"Look, it's flying forwards now."

"It's at no great height at all, though."

"Oh, it's disappeared."

It had indeed gone behind the wall of trees. Before long it returned to its starting place and appeared to repeat the scan of the valley floor.

Gently, Suzy handed Melodie to Monsieur Demille, giving him no time to decline, saying she would be back in a minute.

"I am just popping into the bedroom for something."

As soon as she closed the door, she was on her phone. She collapsed onto the bed and frantically began tapping a message.

CHAPTER 23

Monsieur Demille had no children. At first, holding Melodie, he felt awkward and unsure of what to do. He started to jig her up and down but quickly realised this was not the way to be with a four-year-old. He was an intelligent man beneath his habitual belligerence and soon understood that she was feeling a little frightened and insecure. He tried to explain to her where all the water had come from and why everything had flooded. He seemed to have the knack of telling her unemotionally but in a way she understood, without using baby language. She nodded and smiled at him.

"Will my mummy and daddy be here soon?" she asked again.

He was unsure what to say but reassured her that they would. Putting her down on the floor, he took her hand and led her back to the group who were gathering their blankets around them and reassembling around the fire. Just then, Jerome came in and began to collect yet more coffee cups for washing.

"Dinner will be ready soon," he announced. "I wonder if someone would help Éric set the table?"

Suzy arrived and showed them where the tablecloth was.

Monsieur Demille glanced at his wife and realised she would be of no practical help at all. She was huddled in her own thoughts and not responding to anyone else. He sighed. "I do love her, you know," he whispered to Suzy. "I was attracted first to her vivacity as well as her sparkling eyes when we were young. Sometimes we lose track of these things until something like this happens to remind us how lucky we are."

He turned to Melodie and asked, "Will you help me, young lady? I might get in a muddle without you."

She smiled up at him. They headed to the kitchen to start collecting the necessary cutlery and condiments. On entering the room, he glanced around and heaved a noisy sigh at the disarray that greeted him.

"So, where's all this stuff for the table?" he demanded of Jerome a little gruffly.

Jerome flicked his head in the direction of the old dresser along the far wall but refused to speak to his old adversary. Monsieur Demille found a tray tucked down beside the large piece of furniture, and he and Melodie counted out knives, forks and spoons. He automatically used it as a learning task, and they made a game of it.

Suzy arrived and bent down to kiss the top of Melodie's blonde head. "I'm very proud of you for being so sensible and helpful," she said. "I don't think Monsieur Demille could manage without you." She glanced up at the old man and gave him a smile. "Thank you both."

Everyone gathered around the dining table. Only Jerome was missing. The villagers assumed he would do the serving on his own, as if they were in his restaurant. He was happy to take that role. He was in his element, placing the steaming pots down the centre of the table. The aromas that emanated from the large dishes were powerful, causing all to realise they were very hungry. It had been a long morning.

"Mmm," was the only noise to be heard.

Eventually, Harriet said, "Jerome, your place is here between Jo and me."

"That's alright. I'll have mine in a bit," he replied.

Monsieur Demille harrumphed and waggled his arm in the direction of the empty chair. It was as close as he could come, at that point, to asking Jerome to join the gathering.

The dishes began to circulate, and soon there was more chatter than there had been all morning as people were forced to communicate when passing and receiving things. They were compelled to think of something other than the recent catastrophic events too. There were two bottles of wine on the table as well as a carafe of water and some beer. Whether it was the wine, the food or the general air of co-operation, anyone who might have seen the gathering could have mistaken it for a family reunion or even a party, so animated were people becoming.

Jo caught Harriet's eye and mouthed that she was going to find Suzy. She found her standing by the window and touched her arm with gentle concern. There was no reply. She led Suzy to a chair by the fire. Her phone was in her hand.

"He's not answering," she blurted out. "He's not answering his phone. Why not? I don't know what to do. Who should I ring now? I don't know anyone's number. What if he's injured or…" She couldn't finish the thought.

Jo enfolded her friend. "Shh, shh," she soothed, rocking Suzy as if she were a frightened child. "There could be any number of reasons. He could have dropped it."

Suzy looked at her and frowned. Then her head tilted and her eyebrows rose in a silent question, willing this to be possible.

"I'll get Harriet. She will know what to do. Wait here," Jo said as she thrust a box of tissues at Suzy and hurried from the room.

In the living room, all the diners were much more relaxed, and Jo was able to get Harriet's attention. Harriet could see immediately that she was needed, so she rose from her chair and discreetly followed Jo, listening to her partner's concerns as they approached Suzy.

"We'll phone Pierre le Bec first," Harriet said authoritatively, delving into her pocket for her phone. "I don't have much charge left. I think I've got enough for this and then I'll copy down any other numbers that might be of use just in case it runs out. Suzy, can you fetch a paper and pencil, please?" When Suzy had gone, she added, "At least that'll keep her occupied while I speak with the mayor."

She made the call. "Pierre, it's Harriet." There was a pause. "Yes, we're all fine. Jerome has cooked a wonderful dinner, and everyone is feeling better. But we're really concerned because Suzy cannot contact Jean Chri. He's not answering his phone. Have you seen him recently?"

There was a much longer pause then as Harriet listened. Suzy returned more quickly than Harriet had intended. She turned away, because she realised her expression would give away her reaction to the news she was hearing.

Suzy was watching like an eagle, thinking the worst.

"Thanks, Pierre. Let us know the latest, won't you? Bye." She hung up. "Okay, Suzy. There has been a bit of an accident."

"What? What has happened? Is he alright?"

"I'm sure he will be, but just now no-one is sure where he is. They are out looking for him. That is what the medicopter is doing now. That's why we saw it going back and forth," Harriet said. "Apparently there is a lot more water than we thought, and his tractor got caught up in it."

Harriet's tone was deliberately calm. She omitted to say that Jean Chri's tractor had been seen overturned and tumbling in the torrent. She gave no details about the full extent of the damage and the problem. There would be time enough for that when Jean Chri was found — *if* Jean Chri was found.

"I need to go and help. We need to find him." Suzy's voice rose in her panic.

"Suzy, that's not possible now. Let the people who know what they're doing do it. You're needed here. Melodie needs you. Pierre will let us know as soon as he has news. You need to be here when Jean Chri returns."

"Yes. Okay. I'm panicking." Suzy gasped in some air. "Calm, I must be calm," she muttered to herself.

Suzy intercepted the glance that Harriet gave Jo, and Jo realised instantly that her partner had only told half the story. Her heart thumped. Suzy frowned. She had been Jo's friend for so long, and this friend knew what sacrifices she had made in the past, looking after her mother; not fulfilling her potential when relationships came along and how difficult her life had been at times. Here, she seemed to have found, at long last, a place where she could be completely happy and fulfilled, with a man she had quickly come to adore. Surely this was not going to end in another tragedy.

"As soon as there is news, you will know," Jo urged.

Wearily, Suzy rose from the edge of the chair and the three of them returned to the table. As eyes turned to the gathering, Suzy consciously squared her shoulders and pasted on a calm expression. She smiled her reassurance at her long-time friend and nodded at the others who were seated.

Suzy could not, however, sit still, and she crossed to the window again. She had only been standing there for a moment when she felt a small hand creep into hers. Looking down, she saw Melodie beside her. The little girl leaned against her side.

All the guests were finishing their dinner. Neither Jo nor Harriet said anything about the latest developments. Suzy was grateful since the last thing she needed or wanted was to be fussed around by the many elderly women who were there. She could certainly do without the doom and gloom attitude of Madame Demille, as well.

Jerome was resuming his role as waiter, chef and bottle washer. He was now bringing in coffee to pour into the tiny cups favoured by the French. He placed the jug and a box of sugar lumps on the table.

Just then, Monsieur Demille did a very surprising thing. He stood and cleared his throat and looked awkward. There was silence for several moments. Then, rather grandly, he started to make a little speech of gratitude. Many in the room gaped.

"Jerome, I know we've had our differences, but I just think we should acknowledge that you have given us a lot today. Er, um, thank you," he finished.

With these beginnings of a reconciliation, Jo leaped into action and her bubbly attitude began to encourage the room full of people.

"Charades!" she announced.

There was a groan from some. Others declined firmly and mumbled about being too old or not in the mood. One or two laughed gently but waved her away as if she were a little deranged. Jo, however, refused to take no for an answer, perfectly aware that her name may well be taken in vain later. She was convinced that people needed an activity to distract them.

She went first and managed to mime the name of the well-known French book by Jules Verne, *Twenty Thousand Leagues Under the Sea*. It was a hit-and-miss activity, with Jo holding her nose and pretending to sink under water. Eventually, Alexandre guessed the answer, although he had never read the book. He chose a television programme to mime and one of the elderly ladies, who had declined to play, guessed the answer quite quickly. While not everyone was fully participating, it kept the room amused and entertained.

The two Augustin lads, Alexandre and Nicolas, were a great help to Jo, cajoling, mildly flirting with the elderly ladies and generally keeping the atmosphere light-hearted. Finally, Jo had all the room laughing when she tried to mime the name Trotsky. Even Madame Demille was giggling and shouting out suggestions. The more Jo trotted around the room, the more bizarre the responses became.

"Oh, you English are funny," said Madame Demille. She turned to Alexandre. "*Tu es un personage aussi.*"

"You are a character, too," Harriet translated for Jo.

"You have made me laugh so much I must go to the toilet," Madame Demille added. She shed her blanket and struggled to her feet. All the company chuckled and nodded with understanding.

CHAPTER 24

As the afternoon advanced, Suzy could not help drifting back to the window. She watched the red and yellow medicopter again, sweeping the valley. She imagined the personnel on board scrutinising the riverbanks and the edges of the water. Maybe Jean Chri had managed to crawl to land and was at this moment heading back to her. From what her visitors had said, there were trees down. It must be hard for the people aboard the craft to see a person with all the debris in the water, even from their low altitude.

"Jo, look!" Suzy shouted across to her friend.

It caught the attention of all the people who were chattering animatedly. Yet again they all made their way to the window to witness the drama, unaware of Suzy's inner turmoil.

As they scanned the scene, a man emerged from the side door of the medicopter and descended on a line. He was swinging slightly, and it all looked very fragile.

It seemed like quite a long time later that the winch began to raise the man from below their line of sight. Something else was harnessed to him. Streaming water made it difficult to see. It looked like a person, with arms hanging loose and head to one side.

"What do you think? Who is it? Do you think it's him?" Suzy asked Jo quietly. Tears seeped from her eyes and rolled silently down her cheeks. A deep frown spread across her forehead.

"Right, the rain is easing off again now." Jo spoke decisively. "Alexandre, would you take Suzy down the road in your tractor? See if you can find the mayor, and help her to ask him what is going on."

"Certainly, I shall," the obliging young man answered.

They donned waterproofs and hurried down the steps in the grey drizzle. It was a squeeze in the ancient tractor cab. Perched uncomfortably next to the driver's seat on the wheel arch, Suzy's head was bent and her back thrust against the window. She was glad, though, that it was usual practice for just about all the younger people and many older ones in the village to own such a vehicle.

As they left the driveway and went down the road and around the slight bend, they could not believe their eyes. The once peaceful, friendly little river was unrecognisable. There was water everywhere, rushing and tumbling with a rage that was frightening. As they watched, mesmerised, quite a large tree came careering down the valley, carried by the flood at a furious pace. The house on the far corner was half gone. Its walls had disappeared. The fireplace was hanging out, and it felt somehow obscene to see someone's wallpaper exposed, along with half their furniture and ornaments.

"I don't think even the bridge is there anymore," Alexandre said in a bewildered voice. "It all looks so foreign."

They sat and watched, unsure what to do. Then in the distance, they heard the siren of an emergency vehicle. Then they heard another, and very soon there was a cacophony of sound as the red vehicles came into sight across the water from where they were sitting.

"There, over there," Alexandre said. "I think that's him."

"Who? Where?" Suzy asked. Her heart started thumping.

"Pierre. *Monsieur le Maire.*"

"Oh." Disappointment flooded Suzy's chest.

Before Alexandre could stop her, she flung open the cab door and leaped down into the road. Running towards the surging flood, Alexandre was in hot pursuit and managed to grab her arm before she got too close. He was far more aware of the imminent danger than Suzy was at that moment.

"I must ask where Jean Chri is," she shouted above the noise. She searched her pockets. "How could I have been so stupid? I left my phone."

"I have mine," said Alexandre. "I will phone Pierre for you."

"Thank you so much," Suzy said desperately. She could hear the panic in her own voice.

There were several frustrating minutes while she watched his face, trying to understand his rapid French.

"What is it?" She grabbed his arm as soon as the call was finished.

"They found Jean Chri in the flood. It took them some time to spot him because he was wedged against a tree trunk that has since passed on down the river. Apparently, the trees that came down higher upstream then got stuck across the river and formed a dam. When one broke free, tonnes of water came with it and broke the bank. With the force of it the trees have just crashed through everything; they've taken down the corner of that house and damaged the bridge beyond repair."

"Right! But what about Jean Chri? Is he alright?" Suzy was almost shaking him.

"The medicopter lifted him out and they're taking him to hospital."

"But he's alive? He's alright, isn't he?" Suzy's legs buckled beneath her, and Alexandre just managed to catch her before she fell. She had feared much worse, and her heart was beating so fast she felt dizzy.

"Suzy, I know no more," the poor young lad answered.

"Which hospital?"

"What?"

"Alexandre, to which hospital will they take him?"

"I don't know. There's the one in Arras or the other one near the coast. I don't know. It could even be Amiens, I suppose."

"We must get home. I need to phone around and find him," Suzy shouted as she turned and started to run.

Suzy looked in the *annuaire*. With a fearful urgency, she found the numbers for the more local hospitals. It took her longer than it should have because her hands were still shaking.

She passed the numbers to Alexandre with a pleading look. He seemed the most capable among them and had a presence that seemed to command respect. He took the numbers and once more found his mobile phone.

Again, Suzy was scrutinising Alexandre's expression to gain clues. His first call ended relatively quickly, and he just shook his head ruefully while dialling the next number.

The second call took longer, and Suzy was more hopeful. She heard Jean Chri's name and then his address. There was a long, long pause. Suzy clamped her hands around the back of a chair, her knuckles showing white.

Jo came across and put her arm around Suzy's shoulders, and Suzy placed her hand upon Jo's with gratitude. Finally, the person at the other end of the line returned with news. Standing up straight in her agitation, Alexandre shook his head sadly at Suzy.

"*Rien*," he sighed, spreading his arms and shrugging. "I shall phone for the number at Amiens."

Finally, they tracked Jean Chri down at Amiens, but information was scarce. They were reluctant to divulge anything on the telephone, especially since they were not relatives.

Melodie quickly picked up on Suzy's fretful worry. Truly sorry for this, Suzy hugged the child to her. Melodie began to wail.

"When will mummy and daddy come?"

"*Chouchou, chérie*," Suzy said. "I don't know what is happening at the moment. I do know they love you and they will be happy to know that you are safe here with us. We must all be brave." She turned to Jo. "I must go to Amiens."

"It's an hour's drive, at least. Will it be safe to travel?"

"I have to try. I remember it's main roads all the way, and it's higher ground."

"I think I should come too."

"I don't want to leave Melodie," Suzy said. Tears welled in her eyes.

Jo spoke in English so that the child would not understand. "I know it's not necessarily suitable for her to come to the hospital, but I could look after her there until we know how Jean Chri is. It would take her mind off waiting here for her parents, though, and she might be able to see him."

"What if they come while we are out?"

"They certainly won't mind staying here until we return. At least they will know what is happening, if they arrive. Everyone here will tell them."

"Right, yes. I'll fetch some things for her to do and some snacks she might like. Then we can go," Suzy said. "Oh no! The cows, they will need attention. I know Jean Chri made sure they were alright in the early hours of this morning, but they will need milking or something."

"Will you and Nicolas see to them?" Jo asked Alexandre.

"*Bien sûr*," he answered easily. "*Nous sommes tous de bons voisins. We must be in such times of difficulty.*"

"Yes, that's true, good neighbours indeed, and I think some have become good neighbours again," Suzy acknowledged with a nod across the room. Jerome seemed to be chatting amicably with some of the previously hostile villagers. "Thank you, Alexandre. Thank you so much."

"I'll drive your car," Jo said in a determined voice. "You're not really in a fit state. You can sit in the back with Melodie."

The car journey passed in a blur. Somehow, Jo managed to convince the hospital staff to take Suzy to Jean Chri, while she stayed with Melodie. When Suzy looked into the room through the small window in the door, Jean Chri was sleeping. He looked unshaved and unkempt. They had given him some shapeless thing to wear, but otherwise he looked peaceful. Then she became conscious of the drip entering a vein through his hand, and she couldn't help but put her hand to her mouth. She inhaled sharply.

The young nurse standing beside her put her hand upon Suzy's shoulder and said something about being careful. Suzy didn't understand. Did she mean Suzy or the medical team? Jean Chri had a strange sort of blanket thing around his torso with tubes coming from it. Now that she was here in person, the nurses were more forthcoming.

Suzy gathered that they were unsure if he'd been unconscious or not when they'd lifted him out of the water. He was suffering from severe hypothermia. Apparently, in the medicopter he'd been given air saturated with warm water to help increase the temperature of his core, the nurse said.

"Will he be alright?" Suzy stumbled on the words.

"There is every indication he will be fine. He is responding well. The most dangerous time was the journey here. His heartrate was so low he could have started a cardiac arrhythmia, but that danger has passed. We are bringing his temperature up slowly. We have not had to do an ECLS, or in English I think you call it ECMO, so that's good. That's why he was brought here instead of a more local hospital. We have the capability." The nurse could see she had lost Suzy completely. She tried to explain that an ECMO was something to do with temporarily withdrawing blood, warming it and replacing it.

As they watched, another nurse came to check on Jean Chri. Then she looked across at Suzy's pale, worried face framed in the little window and popped her head around the door. "All will be well," she reassured Suzy. "We will keep him here for a few days to be certain. You can come in, but only for a minute. This is a high dependency area. Really you shouldn't be in here, but I can see how anxious you are."

I wouldn't be able to do this in England, Suzy thought.

"You will be able to see for yourself that he is breathing," the nurse said and smiled.

Suzy walked in. Jean Chri's face looked so normal. Suzy was very relieved as she gently pushed his hair from his forehead and felt some warmth. How she loved this man.

"All will be well. Come back in tomorrow morning. I'm sure you will find a good change," the nurse said in English, for which Suzy was grateful.

She returned to Jo and Melodie to tell them the news. Having telephoned the house and spoken to Harriet, Jo said there was still no sign of Melodie's parents. Was this going to be the next worry?

They decided to go and find a room for the night so that they could visit again in the morning.

"Melodie, would you like a McDo?" Jo asked with enthusiasm.

"Ooh, yes please," she responded. "That's a treat for special occasions, Mummy always says. Will she mind now? Is it a special occasion?"

"Yes, it's a very special time," Suzy said, grinning.

They found themselves a three-bed room in a cheap hotel. Across the road was the fast food restaurant, which they entered eagerly. The food was the same in every country, it seemed, and they settled for complete meals that were familiar.

Melodie was satisfied with the toy that was included with her box of food, and Jo helped her to put it together. Then they spent the next twenty minutes winding the tiny mechanism and racing it across the table.

The next morning, they climbed stairs and walked along hospital corridors, looking for the room to which Jean Chri had been transferred. All hospitals smelled the same, it seemed. Someone in a white coat passed in the opposite direction, nodding a greeting and saying *Mesdames* politely. Two *gendarmes* passed and nodded also, heading for the exit, presumably having completed their business.

Finally, they found the room. Here the patients were in one- or two-bed rooms with a small bathroom and a television. As Suzy opened the door carefully and peeped around, she saw that currently the other bed was empty, for which she was grateful. As silently as possible, she and Melodie walked hand in hand to Jean Chri's side. He was sleeping. As they approached, his eyes slid open and he smiled.

"Suzy, Melodie. My two favourite girls. You will never know how good it is to see you," he mumbled sleepily.

"I do know," Suzy said meaningfully as she bent to kiss his forehead. "We won't stay long. The nurse said you need rest, but we had to come as soon as they would let us. Yesterday you were all wired up, so Melodie couldn't come into the room you were in and I was only allowed a quick look."

"You were here yesterday?"

"Of course," Suzy reassured him. "Jo drove us here. She's waiting just outside the room, now."

He reached for Suzy's hand. There was so much to say. Melodie sat on the edge of his bed and as he put his arm around her, she snuggled into him.

"I have things to tell you," he said, looking meaningfully from Melodie to her. "Perhaps in a few minutes Melodie can keep Jo company." He had tears in his eyes, and Suzy thought he must be exhausted.

After a few moments, Suzy told Melodie that Jean Chri was tired and she took her to Jo, promising to join them soon.

When Suzy returned to Jean Chri, he rolled onto his side, pulling her onto the bed. He cradled her gently, and with tears rolling silently down his face and into her hair, he told her the awful news.

"The *gendarmes* have just been. Oh, Suzy." He paused as his voice broke and he was silent for a moment, holding her tightly. "Melodie is an orphan."

CHAPTER 25

It had been so good to have Jean Chri back home. Following his short stay in hospital, Suzy had collected him and they had gone to his house. Hers was still full of people as the mopping up took place.

The main sewer pipe had been punctured when the riverbank had washed away. Contractors arrived with massive machinery. Jo, Harriet and several of the others had to don contamination suits in order to enter their homes to collect some of their more precious belongings. The structural inspector said it was alright for them to go into their houses, but some of the other villagers' homes were deemed unsafe. Those houses with *torchy* walls were too flimsy if, indeed, the mud and straw was there at all. Those with stone walls had fared slightly better, the lime mortar being more resilient than either *torchy* or cement and blockwork walls of more modern dwellings. Several houses were being razed to the ground. The owners had been assured that rebuilding would advance quickly.

They were having the first meeting of the Regeneration Group. Harriet and Suzy had been asked to be part of this as representatives of the British community in the immediate area. The sun was shining as Suzy walked briskly to the meeting, which was in the *mairie*.

How strange it was to have such fresh, bright weather after what they had experienced. The building they entered, fortunately, had escaped the flood, being just far enough away from the river and on the slight rise that led up to Suzy's house. The room was already quite full of people sitting around a long table. Some she knew well now, but many were strangers.

Suzy moved to greet the people with whom she was familiar, kissing those on each cheek and shaking hands with the others. Finally, she sat between Monsieur Demille and Harriet. She was pleased Harriet was there. She was a friendly face in a sea of formality and uncertainty, although Monsieur Demille was almost a reformed character and was becoming a good friend.

Suzy still had a house full of guests, of whom he was one. They had all come to an agreement regarding finances and living arrangements, however. It was the least she could do for these good people who had lost so much.

The meeting was called to order and Pierre le Bec asked everyone to introduce themselves. There were people from the main services, structural engineers, and various people with construction experience and roles to play in the massive undertaking. The discussion was quite hard for Suzy to follow and she was thankful that Harriet was there beside her. Every so often, when they were getting lost in the technical aspects of the conversation, they were able to whisper a word here and there to each other so that they could catch up.

"I'm glad you are here," Suzy whispered at one stage.

"Likewise," Harriet answered. "It's good of them to include us."

Suzy responded with a smile and a nod. It certainly was. They were clearly a full part of the community now, especially since she was able to help those in need.

"The riverbed has been raised by debris," someone was saying. "The 1 in 10 slope has meant that we estimate seven thousand tonnes of debris has been washed down."

A gasp rippled around the table.

"We shall excavate that. We expect to go one and a half metres down and about three metres across. Well use it to form a new flood defence along each bank of the river."

The next issue referred to was the siting of the two enormous generators and the fuel tanks that had been airlifted in already. Their arrival had caused a stir of excitement. Suzy found her attention wandering from the dialogue as she remembered the thick cables and enormous machinery involved. Even in such a short space of time, a massive amount had been achieved.

"We already have a promise of a grant of 1.2 million euros from the EU," an important-looking man was saying to Pierre le Bec. "This has been a major emergency."

"We have set up an appeal, too," Pierre announced. "Already we have received several hundred euros."

"One of our first priorities will be to restore water and electricity, so we shall be digging 250 metres of trenches first. *Les pelleteuses* are arriving as we speak," the contract engineer was saying.

Suzy had seen an army of digging machines as she'd walked down the road.

"When might this be completed?" Monsieur Demille asked.

"This work should be quite quick. We have already sent cameras down the existing pipework to see where punctures and blockages are, so the water and sewerage will be restored to those properties affected in a few days. All silted-up manholes are being dealt with now. You've probably seen that happening."

There was some more talk about resurfacing roads as the water got beneath the bitumen, causing long-term damage that needed to be mended.

"We will have a separate meeting to support those who are making insurance claims so that house rebuilding can start as soon as possible, and flood damage can be rectified," Pierre said. "The insurance reps are coming later today. I've notified all the people involved."

Suzy glanced at Harriet and she nodded a reassurance. Her claim would be small compared to some, but she had still suffered damage to her internal walls and furniture, and she had lost some of her work in her studio. The cleaning up of mud and sewerage was a horrible task and needed to be done professionally.

Suzy was feeling exhausted from concentrating so hard and trying to follow all that was said. She saw her thoughts reflected in Harriet's face.

"Finally, for today," Pierre was saying, "we need to formally record a massive thank you to all those who turned out to help during the worst of the calamity, especially Jean Christophe Rochefort. He cannot be here today as he is still recuperating, and his farm demands his attention. It's a miracle that more lives were not lost, and it's thanks to those who risked their own safety that this is so. Also, I should like to record my condolences to Jean Christophe for the loss of his brother and sister-in-law. I'm sure everyone here will join me in that."

There was a general murmuring of assent. Suzy lowered her gaze. She still could not meet the looks of others just yet, so raw were her feelings. She felt Harriet's hand creep across to hers and a light squeeze of comfort.

The meeting finished and there was a scraping of chairs as people stood. They milled about for a few moments. Harriet and Suzy expressed their thanks for being included. They exited the *mairie* to head up the hill to Suzy's home.

"The centre of the village is one massive building site. The drain smell gets everywhere, doesn't it?" Harriet put her hand over her nose and mouth.

"Those earth-moving vehicles are enormous," Suzy said. "And it's so strange to see the huge reels of cables, the workmen everywhere and the mud."

"It looks like a small village of caravans, toilet cabins and shower blocks across the valley," Harriet added. "It's all noise — banging, scraping and scooping. I can't help wondering if it will ever be back to normal."

On entering the farmhouse, the sight that greeted Suzy warmed her heart. Jean Chri was sitting by the fire with Melodie curled in his lap. Every time she saw him, she was thankful that he was there, alive and healthy. Melodie had started to suck and chew Choupinette's ears in the last few days, and she had not been smiling. Once or twice there had been major temper tantrums over nothing serious, followed by weeping.

Jean Chri had done the minimum that was necessary for the animals at the farm since Suzy had collected him from hospital. He had been very tired, but she was so relieved to have him back with no further complications. Alexandre and Nicolas had continued to help out, fitting it around their own work.

Melodie and Jean Chri somehow needed to learn to live with their loss, and they were helping each other. Suzy sometimes felt a little useless in that respect.

She had telephoned all her prospective holiday visitors to explain that she couldn't accommodate them for several months. Everyone had heard of their misfortune. It had been on national and even international news programmes. All were very understanding and kind.

Jean Chri and Suzy ensured Melodie was tucked up under her new covers beneath the princess canopy, and then they curled up together in Jean Chri's bed.

"You have become my life," he whispered into her hair. "When everything has been dark, you've been here to rescue me. We'll get through this together, won't we?"

Suzy gave her reassurance with ease. "I don't want to be anywhere else, ever."

They heard soft sobbing and leaped out of bed to rush into Melodie's room. She had not awoken and was crying in her sleep. Jean Chri stroked her forehead and rubbed her tummy until the nightmare passed. Suzy sat quietly with her arm around him. This was not the first time it had happened. Since the funeral, she had had several upsetting dreams. The doctor assured them that it would pass, and that it was early days for her to understand and accept such a great loss. Only Jean Chri truly understood how she was feeling, and as her guardian he would be there for her always.

He'd told Suzy a little about the car being washed downstream, and she'd had only her imagination to help her understand what he saw and felt. "It seems they must have set out in their car quite early and been overtaken by sudden floodwater as the dams of trees gave way. When the car was finally found, they were still inside," Pierre le Bec had told them.

Suzy had known Jean Chri would flay himself in weeks to come for what had happened. "In truth, there was nothing more you could possibly have done to prevent the tragedy. That part was already complete by the time you saw the car," she'd told him.

Both he and Melodie would be angry in time, and would still question whether more could have been done to avoid the situation that had caused the deaths of Pascal and Amélie. Eventually, they would come to terms with the loss. Didn't Suzy know all this? Wasn't it all too familiar? She had witnessed the death of both her parents. All she could do was be there for Jean Chri and Melodie.

There was a lighter side to the healing of their family and their village.

Madame Demille had found a sense of humour eventually and had told everyone how she had been pestering her husband for a water feature in the middle of their lawn before the flood.

"Yes," he said. "She wanted one of those huge dolphin or fish things with water coming out of its mouth."

"I got a bit more than I bargained for with that one." She laughed.

Suzy went with Jo to visit her and Harriet's house and found three large fish on the lawn. Sadly, they were past their best. "I didn't think we would need them for dinner," she had smiled at Harriet.

Jerome told Suzy he got Éric to drive him to the market as it was finishing, just before midday each Friday. He managed to chat to various stallholders about the villagers' trials and tribulations, and so returned with boxes and boxes of donated produce each week. Some of it was past its prime, but much was fit for use and he continued to come up each day and cook for the crowd at Suzy's house. His cellar had been flooded but his house was unscathed, and the rabbits, chickens, turkeys and ducks had all survived; the birds had flown up into the bushes and stumpy trees.

All the villagers were very complimentary about both his cooking and his generosity of spirit. Even the Demilles were helpful, pleasant and friendly. Monsieur Demille was still pernickety and never failed to state his point of view, but everyone either ignored him or shouted him down rather than letting him get his way. He was learning to accept that he was not always right about everything. Generally, they all jogged along well together.

CHAPTER 26

Two years passed quickly enough. All the villagers were back in business. So much had been achieved with quiet determination.

Suzy was walking down the street in the gentle sunshine. At the bridge, she stopped to stare down into the burbling, gentle water and could not help remembering. The old bridge had been replaced with this wider and slightly higher one. The raised flood defences were covered in colour. One tonne of flower bulbs had been donated, and an army of late summer and autumn visitors had volunteered their time to plant them alongside the villagers. Now the heads of the late flowering ones were bobbing their bright colours in the breeze. It was such a warming sight.

This is all something that should be celebrated, Suzy thought, turning her mind to the grand parade and day of fun that was coming up soon.

Visitors to the village could not believe the photographs of the devastation that hung in Jerome's newly refurbished restaurant. He hadn't qualified for much insurance money, but the general regeneration had inspired him to take himself in hand. Behind the scenes he was still chaotic, he still wore the same old apron, but his restaurant was so busy that people needed to book several weeks in advance for a Saturday night or Sunday lunchtime.

Instead of the long table with the tree trunk underneath there was a range of individual tables and beautiful bright white tablecloths. He had painted the walls and there were red and white check curtains at the windows, replacing the slightly grey voile that covered them before.

Nicolas and Alexandre Augustin still called in for a beer after work, but Monsieur Demille was seen just as often in the bar at lunchtimes. He was as dogmatic as ever at times, but he and Jerome could often be heard having a heated but friendly exchange, or sharing a rude joke and laughing together.

Sometimes Éric was seen to display a flash of initiative, although Jerome still needed to tell him what to do a lot of the time. Or perhaps he just liked to tell him, and Éric put up with it. He helped around the place, quietly getting on with things.

Just as she was reflecting on this, Suzy passed Jerome in the street. Shielding his eyes from the sun, Jerome told her his latest news.

"We have a tribunal next week. They are to determine if Éric is well enough to handle his own affairs; his own money and so on."

"How do you think it will go?" Suzy asked.

"I've had to give written evidence," he explained. "I have said I think he will manage now."

"That's really good news."

"Yes, life is much easier these days." Jerome smiled at her. "Changing the subject, how are the preparations coming on for the parade?"

"Very well, I think. We have the children's fancy dress organised with lots of entries promised, and all the stalls are booked for the entertainment. Melodie is determined to go dressed as Little Miss Sunshine, which is appropriate, but we're working on that." Suzy smiled. "How is your food stall coming along?"

"It is good. I have everything ordered and the ladies who do the church flowers are all helping me serve on the day. I've even got Monsieur Demille signed up for cooking the chips. *Monsieur le Maire* has said we can use the tables and chairs from the *Salle des Fêtes* and *le bricoleur* will set them up. All we need is fine weather. It would be so much better to be outside rather than indoors."

"It certainly would, especially since we are celebrating our regeneration after the flood."

"How are your other preparations coming along?" Jerome gave Suzy a wink.

"I'm giving nothing away." She laughed. "All I'll say is that everything has fallen into place now."

He kissed her cheeks. "*Bon, à bientôt, ma petite,*" he added affectionately as he took his leave.

Suzy walked on with a lightness of step. She was heading to Madame Demille's house to collect some vegetables. Suzy had tried her hand at growing produce but she hadn't done so well, despite Jean Chri's advice. She'd had too much else to do, and recently she'd felt sick each morning. On arriving, she glanced across at the front lawn and giggled at the small pool; a large stone fish rose from the centre, with water spurting from its mouth.

At midday, Suzy met the school bus outside the *mairie*. Melodie came bouncing down the steps with a painting in her hand and gave Suzy a hug as she admired her handiwork. Suzy was still finding it hard to say goodbye to her each morning, but Melodie was old enough to go to the little school in the next village now and she was settling in well. Sometimes she was pensive but, overall, she was happy and danced everywhere again. They talked about her mummy and daddy quite often. She had their picture in her bedroom in the farmhouse.

They lived there full-time now, but Suzy had kept the bed and breakfast business going. It suited them well. Jean Chri still worked long hours, and Suzy needed something of her own to do. With that, and looking after the three of them — soon to be four — she was happily occupied.

The morning of the festivities dawned bright and clear. Suzy was so relieved. She had been watching the *météo* every day for a week or more. This was a special day, and not just because of the village celebration. It was Suzy's and Jean Chri's wedding day.

They were to be married at the *mairie*, and then the whole village — plus any tourists — would come together for a momentous parade and a day of celebration, to remind themselves how lucky they were.

There were no guests for Suzy to worry about this week, so she had awoken in her old bedroom. It was still quite early, and the shutters were open for the night-time stars and the morning light. The shadows of the forsythia bushes outside were dancing on her walls. Melodie was in the room next door. Suzy peeped in on her, and she was still fast asleep.

Jean Chri and Suzy had agreed to have one night apart in the old tradition. Melodie and Suzy were to get ready at the B&B, and Jean Chri would get dressed at the farmhouse.

Jerome, Jo and Harriet were coming to meet them just before eleven o'clock, and they would walk down the road together to meet Jean Chri. Then they would all arrive at the *mairie* together. After finally rising, Suzy was too excited to eat but she made a cup of tea and took it outside. It was so mild and still. A blackbird was sitting on the top of the roof and singing in mellow, liquid and effortless tones. It was a perfect sound on a perfect day.

I never dreamed that I could feel so complete, Suzy thought, and she sighed with happiness.

"Suzy, where are you?" She heard the high-pitched voice calling her name.

"I'm out here, *ma chérie*," she responded, rising to take her cup indoors and to greet Melodie with a kiss.

"It's today, at last," she smiled back at Suzy. "It's been ages coming, and now it's here."

The morning was going by quickly. Suzy had washed and brushed Melodie's hair until it was shining and beautiful. She helped her with her dress. It was a shade of sky-blue, to match her eyes, with a cream sash There were small yellow daisies sewn to the skirt here and there. The cream lace collar framed her little face and bright cheeks. In her hair, she had a small crown of the same daisies. Suzy looked at her and smiled.

I love her more than I can describe to myself or anyone else, she thought.

Suzy was ready to put on her own dress. She had chosen the same cream lace and had added a blue satin ribbon around her waist, the exact same shade as Melodie's dress.

The swelling to come was still not showing, but she placed a hand on her stomach protectively anyway.

The dress fitted her frame, and the godets in the skirt gave a flattering swirl below her hips. She had the same crown of bright daisies in her hair and in her bouquet were sunflowers. Melodie and she stood together in front of the old-fashioned cheval mirror. The little girl slipped her hand into Suzy's and looked up at her.

"You look lovely," she said artlessly.

"We both look very fine," Suzy responded. "Are we ready, do you think?"

Melodie nodded.

Just then, there was the clang of the bell at the door. Suzy quickly slipped her feet into her low-heeled cream shoes.

Answering the door, she was surprised and delighted to see who was there. Standing and smiling and in her very best dress and coat was Madame Marie. They had spoken on the phone regularly, but Suzy had thought she would not be able to get there for her wedding. It was a long way to travel, and she was elderly.

"Oh, I'm so pleased to see you," Suzy cried. "I thought you couldn't make it."

They greeted each other with a kiss, but then Madame Marie drew Suzy to her and hugged her generously. "My dear Suzy, you look so lovely." Suzy could have sworn there were tears in her eyes.

Breaking off a bud from her bouquet, Suzy slipped it through Madame's buttonhole. It meant a lot that she was there.

At that moment, the bell rang again. Upon opening it, Suzy was touched again by the sight of Jerome with Jo and Harriet on either side of him, their arms tucked through his. He was newly shaved, and to her great surprise he was in a suit with a white shirt and grey tie. She had never seen him look so smart.

"Well, are you ready?" he asked.

Melodie had arrived at Suzy's side and when she looked down at her fondly, she could see that the child could barely contain her excitement. She nodded and beamed.

Taking Melodie's hand and stepping out into the sunshine, Suzy started down the steps, with Jerome escorting Madame Marie. Jo and Harriet followed behind them. They made a smart, proud little parade of their own.

As Melodie and Suzy arrived at the bottom of the steps, an unexpected sight greeted them. All the way down the street, both sides were lined with people from the village. Spontaneously, the women all began waving sunflowers and the men started clapping until the air was filled with sound. As they passed, the people fell in behind Jo and Harriet. The sound turned to singing behind them, and Suzy could not think of a better accompaniment.

Then, at the end of the triumphant parade, Suzy saw Jean Chri. As she arrived by his side, she could see the light of love in his dark eyes. Melodie took both their hands.

They were together, as a family.

A NOTE TO THE READER

Dear Reader,

Thank you so much for choosing to read *Sunflowers for Suzy*. People who know me will also be familiar that I lived in France for several years. I know the hills and steep-sided valleys in which this book is set, and I'm a sucker for the feelgood experience of living among the sunflowers. There is something so jubilant and heart-warming about the expanses of these joyful flowers ... or is it the memory of warm sun, family visiting, and lying by the pool?

Our neighbours were varied, with some eccentric characters including one who ran a restaurant and heated the room with a tree trunk which really did run under the long table down the centre of the room and into the fire! Nevertheless, we had happy times there with a glass of rich red wine. With such a diverse cast of people in our village, there were historical feuds between families, the origins of which were long forgotten, but still persisted. In this story I invented a scenario that would bring people together, overcoming their differences and helping each other in a time of catastrophe.

I used research about the physical aspects of a great flood which occurred in Boscastle on Monday, 16th August 2004. However, all of the events and characters are from my imagination and the things the restauranteur does are as fictional as all the other events in the story.

If you enjoyed reading *Sunflowers for Suzy*, perhaps you might leave a brief review on **Amazon** or **Goodreads**. It doesn't need to be long; a couple of sentences will more than suffice. It will inform readers when choosing a book and would be a huge boost to this author. Thank you.

If you would like to know more about my writing, my website is **www.rosrendleauthor.co.uk**. Here you can also **sign up for my newsletter** where I often offer free gifts and timely access and information about forthcoming books. I'd love to hear from you, my dear reader, and you are able to chat with me via **Facebook** or via **Twitter.**

Of course, none of this would be possible without the incredible skill of the team at Sapere Books, so it's with huge grateful thanks to each of them for transforming my scribblings into this book.

Thank you, again, and I hope we will meet again soon through the pages of one of my other books.

Ros Rendle

Sapere Books is an exciting new publisher of brilliant fiction and popular history.

To find out more about our latest releases and our monthly bargain books visit our website: **saperebooks.com**